DESPERATE MEASURES

Desperate Measures

JAMES HANNAH

Southern Methodist University Press
Dallas

First Edition, 1988
Requests for permission to reproduce material from this work
should be sent to:
Permissions
Southern Methodist University Press
Box 415
Dallas, Texas 75275

Library of Congress Cataloging-in-Publication Data

Hannah, James.
    Desperate measures.

    (Southwest life & letters)
    Contents: Auto-da-fé—Junior Jackson's parable—
Breaking and entering—[etc.]
    I. Title. II. Series.
PS3558.A4762D47   1988   813'.54   87-26404
ISBN 0-87074-262-0

Grateful acknowledgment is made to the following journals for permission
to reprint: *Cimarron Review* for "Hello to Hello"; *Crazyhorse* for
"Breaking and Entering," "Field of Vision," and "Reefs"; *Florida
Review* for "Sleet"; *Great River Review* for "The Necropolis at
Savoca" and "Three Houses"; *Quarterly West* for "Auto-da-fé."

Designed by Whitehead & Whitehead

To
Cecelia, Velma, and Dave

In memory of Blaine Moulding

Contents

DESPERATE MEASURES

Auto-da-fé

AUGUST. Their dirty U-Haul edged into Columbia at the end of a parade. They crept under a white banner strung between telephone poles. "Annual Watermelon Thump" was spelled out in crudely drawn orange sections of melon a foot high. Just ahead of them a posse of Shriners fought nervous Shetland ponies through complicated moves. The old men's shined shoes scraped the pavement.

Susan leaned out the window, her wind-burned hand and arm on the mirror support. Mexican women held up children and talked and pointed at them as if they were the last entry, some sort of attraction themselves. She smiled and waved a weary arm. Steven honked the horn at the trailing pack of teenagers who darted back and forth in front of the Ford's high grill. Some rushed away to the curb and perched there like herons, one leg tucked under them. A couple shot them the finger. She heard Steven growl through his teeth.

She was glad to be here. She was ready to get unpacked and the house set up and then to explore all the small town's shops and stores and restaurants. She wished she had candy— she would toss it from the windows to the few parents and children too tired just then to follow the tail end of the parade towards the town square.

"Think you can sell those old bastards some new herbicides?" she asked and touched the windshield with her burgundy nail.

Steven shook his head as he followed her gesture to the row of old men — caps advertising diesel power and auto parts stores — sitting on a spindly bench under an oak. "Probably not."

Just ahead, the square opened up. The ugly 1950s courthouse hid itself behind big oaks and ash. People milled from booth to booth; broad piles of melons sandbagged the whole curb. In a dozen places someone had split melons and the red watery flesh was covered with black mists of flies. The pink juice had flushed over curbs and muddied the gutter.

"This is great, isn't it? Really wonderful. Our first real job." She wanted to open the door of the slow truck and step out into the throng of backs and faces.

"Oh, it's great alright. Just great."

But Susan ignored the dangerous undertow of his voice. She wouldn't be pulled under by his fears of the new job. He'd plucked the notice for a chemical rep off the department's bulletin board and gone down to Austin and done quite well in the interview. So she'd skim the surface of his fear and expect it to settle out after the strain of packing and long hot distances retreated.

They had been married three years. She hadn't wanted to finish her degree, so she'd worked in interlibrary loan until Steven had graduated. She had great faith in him, in the power of a degree, in the prospects of those horizons where goals are established and achieved eventually though she knew, her parents had told her, much suffering had to invade the foreground. She expected setbacks. A year ago she'd forced out a red fist of a thing between fish and person. And she'd cried for a whole week afterwards though a child would have been a cruel surprise.

Free of exams, his grumpiness and fear would dissolve in the face of hard work. She knew hard work was the greatest liberator from sulking spells and fits of sleep. Everyone said that. It was what had saved her after the miscarriage. She'd painted and cooked meals from all her exotic cookbooks until they lived in all-new pastels and had gained ten pounds.

Obviously the people here believed in hard work, knew how good it was. They bought and sold and took part. That's what she wanted now—to take part in the world beyond cranky graduate students and the hard grind of school lived through her husband.

Steven kept his palm on the horn until they were out the other side of the crowded square and had turned left on Frio Street south towards their small rented house.

Though they'd flown down only once, and stayed in the Holiday Inn for three days until they'd found the house, as they lumbered down the wide street she felt she was coming home. And she was sure that this was the right feeling to have; that it was there as it should be made her smile and stare past the bug-clotted windshield.

September. Steven kept the St. Augustine grass at the base of the chain link fence so short that it died. And when a neighbor's dog chewed a limb off the young maple in the front yard he clipped it to the ground a foot at a time, branch by branch.

Susan saw him from the bedroom window. Fascinated, she crouched low at the windowsill and turned her ear to the screen. The early fall day, the first slight chill hiding almost successfully behind the full sunlight, was full of Saturday morning noises. She saw his mouth move, its corners puckered and ugly. But even with her ear pressed into the screen so that its silver mesh bowed out taut, she couldn't hear his voice. Only the snick of the anvil clippers reducing the tree to ruler-length twigs.

Later she asked him about the tree, about what had happened to it. And Steven looked at her over the table and then looked down and smiled lamely. "I got carried away, I think. That damned dog really set me off and I hacked it down." He had looked up then into her eyes. "I'll get another and we'll put it out, okay?"

She knew he wasn't very successful at work so far. But she was sure it was simply because he didn't work quite hard enough yet. He was out by 7:30 and home by 5:30 even when he drove miles into the country. He didn't seem to push himself very much. But he argued that this time of year wasn't the best for selling any sort of ag chemicals really. She took his word for it; he should know. But she knew he'd never had a job before except an assistantship in his department. She had seen him in the library several times before they were married, before they'd even met. He'd been bent over books. But passing behind him unnoticed, she'd seen the pages of doodles—loops and spirals and runaway caricatures. Her own father had died at work. And Steven's father refused to retire.

After all, he was fine at the company's six-week training school. And he was young and could learn. One had to learn to work, she supposed. And if things were so bad, he could use his energy to change them. He would become an excellent salesman.

Things would change. They would get better. If you kept busy and talked about the problems then they would work out. She had learned this somewhere. Or maybe she'd read it, though as advice it seemed too simple for the things that filled daytime shows and newspaper columns. Her mother hadn't said it. Her mother viewed the world completely differently. So maybe she had learned it from her in a way—the same way you learn to raise children by avoiding how couples you know raise theirs.

October. Steven went to the small office near the railroad tracks later in the morning now. And for the first time they argued in adult tones and used the collected and distilled vehemence they hadn't realized was there.

"Then work harder. Get out and line up some business for the spring," she yelled, aware that on this first really cold morning the bathroom window was open. She glanced out and across the narrow side yard to the Rankins' closed windows.

"Get a goddamned job yourself," Steven shouted back, the electric shaver buzzing in his clenched fist.

And on it went through the one month most cherished in Columbia because in it the heat lifted like an oppressive dream from the landscape of stony pastures and black pumping units and useless mesquite. It brought football weather and men smiled more and women took out of cedar chests heavy expensive wool pants.

Susan cried in the car on the way to Wal-Mart. And she shook her head when she checked their savings account balance and learned that the whole month, now almost gone, had been paid for with her tedious hours over the typewriter at the mercy of distraught graduate students' failing thesis topics.

But she didn't call her mother, though as she cooked or vacuumed or raked the broom overhead in corners, she considered the peace of her childhood. And she wondered what advice there was to be had. She conjured her mother's voice until it became a daily companion, until by mid-afternoon, when she went outside to bring in her ferns, it had become a tiresome drone of fragments from her youth: admonitions about good grades; warnings about boys' hands. Nothing applicable to husbands and quarrels.

Yet in remembrances of her childhood she readily took comfort from an already frequented world where boys hadn't yet fumbled between her legs and becoming a tennis champion was still a certainty.

November. Thanksgiving they visited his parents in Little Rock and ate early dinner at Luby's—his mother no longer cooked big meals, she said. Then he and his father walked along the river and came home to figure for an hour or two on canary-yellow legal pads on the den's glass-topped coffee table.

In front of his parents they never stopped touching one another.

Then at home the figuring continued as the cold set in for good finally, even this far south. The sky was azure and the north-facing pipes froze hard. A faucet burst.

Sunday she rose and went to church for the first time in a dozen years. She drove cautiously past the Lutheran church, the ingoing stragglers clutching coats against the chill, and she pulled into the First Baptist parking lot. She'd really wanted to go elsewhere but despite her alienation from the vengeance of Baptists' literal hell and their too dim heaven, she thought Catholics and Methodists and all the others as foreign as Moslems.

Susan sat through the service. And no time had passed at all. The booming voice from the spindly minister rolled out the key to eternal salvation. God works in mysterious ways; grinds slow but exceedingly fine. And five ideas all beginning with the letter W.

At dinner she talked to Steven about the nice organ music; she recalled their marriage and his parents' gift—the honeymoon suite with mirrored ceilings.

But he rushed from the table and then came immediately back with a wad of paper which he smoothed out between their dirty plates.

His chewed pencil trailed down the columns; he looked straight at her. She tried following his steady voice but at the end of each scribbled row she was dumbfounded by it all.

"Dad agrees completely. The money's there and now I can get it. Granddad'd be proud we used it this way, don't you see?"

But thirty acres seemed a universe to her. She recalled his reluctance to mow this small yard. She saw him butchering the maple months ago.

"Why not in town, then?" She ran a finger around the edge of a plate.

Steven smiled and tipped the chair back.

"Or after the business really takes hold?"

And Steven leaned forward over the pages and started in again with interest rates and itemizing and wait until you see it, it's perfect. And on he gabbed about chickens and dogs and sunsets and quiet and challenges thick and fast. So much hovered in the air she thought she might choke long after their meal and talk.

Under the edge of the house the next truly cold spell, she wrapped the old *Newsweeks* around the pipes while he swaddled them in silver duct tape. In the dim light Susan sympathized with the pipes. Later their sputtering groans produced slivers of ice in the lavatory as fragile as glass.

She promised a decision. And she gave one soon after they'd struggled in the lip of light at saving a hot bath. She'd move. She promised herself she'd find some way to help him out. And she swore she'd keep her mind off churches.

December. Business would almost always come to a big slow-down during the winter, Steven pointed out. No farming, no need for pool chemicals. But he had some great plans for spring. They'd just use a little of Granddad's money to get by on. So he limited his Christmas present to a fancy clock radio that brought in the Austin stations forty miles away. And she gave him a down vest. "For field work," she'd said.

And two days after Christmas they'd driven outside town five miles to look at the land. The house wasn't so bad really. The old man who'd lived there had tried his best, Susan supposed. But the bathroom was awful, as if he'd never paid it any attention. There were holes in baseboards from mice. And wherever he'd made repairs, edges didn't quite meet and wiring dangled behind cupboard doors.

The outside was much the same. The front yard, bare of trees, wasn't much larger than the small porch. And the backyard was a maze of wire pens for his dogs, who'd worn bald spots everywhere. The one tree was an ancient chinaberry that littered the porch with soft, smelly berries. The adjacent fields were choked with mesquite.

And it all was dominated by the gigantic barn that shared the small rise with the house. It was a patchwork of tin and wood, a map of the old man's life out here.

Steven had been out before, some customers having told him of the old man's death and his relatives' desire to sell.

Now, facing into the frigid wind, they approached the barn from the house. Susan watched Steven stride ahead of her, his arms outstretched to encompass the rambling thing. The wind whipped the top of the rise — Steven called it a hill — and loose tin hummed. They stopped at the exposed stalls along one side. A huge rusted bulldozer was hemmed in by tall dead weeds. A shelf overhead was crammed with starters and generators. Spark plugs littered the ground at their feet like some weird seed.

Steven patted the blade of the Caterpillar. "Everyone tells me this is worth a thousand easy. And if I could get it to start. . ." He nodded his head. "And these," he stepped through the weeds to the corroded shells of the generators, "maybe ten bucks apiece." He trampled the Johnson grass and took Susan by the elbow. "And wait'll you see inside."

In the dim light from dirty windows they edged past piles of everything: toasters and waffle irons, the guts of dozens of TVs. The immense cavern of the barn was filled with piles of junk. She'd never been so surrounded by useless things and while Steven talked on she stopped and bent to look out a broken pane.

The tiny house could be mended with the right touches. It wouldn't be so bad giving in to him on this. He seemed amazed that he could own all these things.

January. The unusual warmth gave way to severe weather. The road that turned off the asphalt highway was all iron puddles and ridges.

Susan learned to watch from windows; she rediscovered in herself—when she surveyed the barn through narrowed eyes—that sly, secretive twelve-year-old whose parents shook their heads over sneaked cookies and pitchers of Kool-Aid refilled with tap water.

At the first rush of cold wind she'd brought out hot coffee, the steam rising towards the greasy rafters. Steven had swept clear a circle a few feet wide. A wall of junk rose beyond the weak light of the one clear bulb.

"Need a hand, don't you?" She eyed the dull mounds of things and saw lines of attack. The house she'd put in order as their failing money allowed. Despite the dark corners and heavy objects she was anxious to pitch in here too.

Steven stood from squatting in front of an old TV, withdrawing his hand that had been thrust deep into its back. His fingers emerged clenching a web of wires; a tube fell to the floor and rolled off unbroken.

"Coffee's a fine idea. Here. . ." and he maneuvered her to a high bench under a dirt-fogged window. The chilled light outside lay across the nose of the bulldozer.

"I love this work out here." Steven smiled and inhaled deeply and drank the coffee down. He smacked his lips and nodded. "A guy came by yesterday. . ."

"For an order?"

Steven shrugged. "Maybe in the spring. Anyway, I mentioned all this stuff and he said the real money was in the copper wire. Think of all the generators out here."

He worked late and she decided to watch TV. But a few days later she poked open the door to dip out a cup of chicken scratch for the Rhode Island Reds she'd bought and she stepped inside. The cleared circle seemed smaller. Bending, she examined the narrow aisle near the door. The splotched brown floor was gashed open, long fresh gouges exposing the yellow pine. The floor of the circle looked as if animals had clawed and furred the soft wood. He'd dragged something here; her eyes led her to a smashed air conditioner. But there were two sets of marks. Straightening, Susan realized that everything had been moved and then returned. The expectant chickens clucked at the door. It was silly to keep her eye on him when he seemed so happy and busy. She believed that having finished with the house for now, all she needed was a good long novel for the cold days. She watched reruns of the Summer Olympics.

February. What's to be done when we really must do something? she wondered.

The first knock that morning was him returning to sit on the cane-bottomed chair near the bed. His fingers reached for her cheek. Susan turned the bruises away and looked down at her cluttered end table.

"Things *are* better," he said. His voice a hush from a few minutes ago. Then it had rattled the window by the bureau. "And I'm not acting weird, as you say. I've got a lot on my mind...the business...everything out here."

She watched him look out the window at the leafless mesquite. "There's a lot to do." He was silent and then he shrugged.

Susan stared. Her cheek ached where he'd slapped it in the bathroom. She'd never been hit before. Not by hands or anything. From the headboard she could just see the trailing cord of the clock snaking over the threshold. Its shattered face in long plastic splinters. She had never feared a person before.

Then toward ten another knock. She got stiffly out of bed, avoided the jagged clock pieces, and answered the door.

Phil Burke stepped in out of the cold wind. He looked at her face and she combed her fingers through her oily hair. She left her hand at her cheek.

"He sent me back for some checks, missy."

Susan sat in the small vestibule, no bigger than a closet. Phil Burke took a crumpled bunch of envelopes from his work-jacket pocket and Susan reached and took them.

Dumbly she wrote out the checks. Her signature stopped her every time. Susan E. Cameron, she wrote. But the ball-point rested on the final letter. This woman here, she thought. She'd never been hit. Not by her father. Not by her mother or by hands or with any object. And as she signed them and handed them up to the tall stoop-shouldered man who twisted an old felt hat in his hands, she passed away that more fortunate woman.

"He's got some good ideas," Phil Burke said to her at the door. "But. . . anyway, he'll do just fine this spring. You'll see."

After he'd gone into the wind that forced him to crush the hat low over his eyes, she went to the unheated living room and lay on the couch.

A week ago she'd started to talk to Maria at the beauty shop in town. But all around her women gabbed to women about men, wives complained. Susan's reflection looked idiotic in the mirror, her wet hair plastered in silly ringlets across her forehead. Maria chattered on as Susan looked as deeply into her own eyes in the mirror as she possibly could. He's bitten off too much. That's all.

And she'd driven past the Baptist Church again. She'd parked in front of Our Lady of Guadalupe and watched the young Hispanic priest hurry, burdened with trays of food, from his kitchen to the small white school behind the stone church. He looked kind and young like untried priests in movies who either crumple at the first hard blow or rise up inhuman in power and will. She'd never talked to a priest before; she'd never had friends who were Catholic.

There were no places to phone.

Almost asleep on the couch, the wind sheering off the north face, she rose at the third knock.

This man was small and neat, his blue uniform and quilted coat tucked tightly in at his waist. The eyelids drooped halfway over his brown irises. She saw a throat as thin as the priest's and as brown.

The water bottles at his feet caught the light and tossed it upward against the two of them in quivering circles.

"Mrs. Cameron?" He grinned and looked down at his notebook. "You wanted to start with Agua Dulce water?"

Susan nodded, her hand to her left cheek again. The bottles gathered all the light in the front yard.

"Had enough of this awful local stuff, huh?"

Susan only cried for a moment, her hands moving from her cheek to her eyes and on up to her forehead. And when the Agua Dulce man came in and made coffee from his newly opened bottle, he moved more naturally around her kitchen than she did.

March. By his fourth delivery they shouldered a bottle apiece and began dripping the thick coffee beforehand so the aroma filled the bedroom.

Afterwards he would read the newspaper. Often he'd read her an article about college or pro basketball. He couldn't believe she knew so little and it delighted him to quiz her about previous stories.

She liked their time together, their idle chatter that reminded her of dates years ago in high school. But if she thought long enough she couldn't understand what she expected to come of it.

He never pried into her life, but if she talked, he folded away the paper and listened.

April. Susan held tight to the windowsill and the Agua Dulce man entered her anus with a sudden shove that made her eyes water. This was something new for her. He had wanted it for some time and finally she didn't care enough to keep batting him away.

As he worked behind her she dug her nails into the soft rotting pine and pressed her forehead against the cool screen. She looked out at the barn. One side Steven had painted barn-red with a brush a foot wide. But near the eaves he'd been frustrated by trailing globs of birds' nests and early yellow jackets. He'd moved to the roof and sloshed aluminum paint on the tin with a mop. But last week he'd slipped and rattled down the tin and she'd come to the back door in time to see him flow spread-eagled over the edge and land with a thump just a foot from the bulldozer blade.

For a long time she stood at the door and waited until she saw him rise to his knees and then she walked out to him and sat on the blade despite its deep flaking rust.

"I think I've sold three generators," he said as he rose shakily and felt his left arm.

"I've got an application in with the phone company," she'd said and risen. But he'd taken two steps and put his dusty hand down on her shoulder.

The last twitch was tiny and weak but he stayed deep inside her and Susan felt his breath as he hunched over her and rested his chin on her shoulder. Then she felt him run his fingers over the round bruises that spotted her back like sugar splotches on overripe fruit. He outlined them and finally pulled away and lay heavily on the bed.

The cool air was pleasant on her face and cold where his sweat coated the small of her back and hips. As she lay back she felt his semen run down her leg.

May. Though he brought them water only twice a month, the Agua Dulce man altered his route so he could stop by every week.

Once, Phil Burke had knocked and Susan had gone to the door with only her robe on. But the water man always stopped down the lane and backed into an old pasture road no one used.

And one time, as she'd gripped the window frame — she'd scratched grooves in the pine over the last two months — she choked to see Steven drive up in the company pickup and get out at the barn.

"Hey!" Susan yelled at him. Behind her the movement stopped.

Steven turned and waved and pulled open the sagging barn door. She'd watched him bring out two rusted generators and drop them into the truck bed. But he'd only waved again over his shoulder. And with the last noise of the truck on the gravel drive the activity behind her started with renewed vigor.

Susan shifted on the hard kitchen chair, her anus unbearably sore. The Agua Dulce man filled the kettle.

"You should leave him, then," he said over his shoulder as he measured the coffee into the white paper filter.

Susan was glad when they were gone. She was pleased when they'd both finished with her and the road was silent and she'd opened all the windows and the attic fan sucked the last smell of the coffee away.

"I don't think he'd let me now," she answered the Agua Dulce man toward the end of the month.

"I could help you. You could just pack up and I'd see you off."

Susan shook her head over the hot coffee. She was sure he would leave the business, the barn, and his land long enough to drive after her. He'd only have to search a few places. People can't just go anywhere they want.

June. The Agua Dulce man may have had a wife. Or maybe not. Susan thought that he loved his job. That bringing good water to replace the smelly white liquid from the oil-soaked water table was a mission of sorts that replaced his high school athleticism. He loved all that water talk—dissolved salts and solids; ionized and distilled—and he loved stock car races.

"We'll go sometime. To Austin, what do you say?"

Susan nodded for him. It was such an impossible idea.

"Maybe you should kill him?" he'd said, pulling on his tight blue jacket. "Maybe that's the answer," and he reached out and picked up the newspaper and rattled the front page. "Like this woman here done." He shook it again. "He was mean to her too."

After she'd changed the sheets and crammed them in the washer, she walked out into the living room and sat and turned on the radio. She had a teardrop crystal hanging from the curtain rod. She watched it turn in the warm breeze and the light of the near-noon sun streaked the walls yellow and blue. She went over to the clearest, largest swath and tried to pick out the more subtle colors. Maybe I should, she told herself. She feared every moment with him now. She recalled his young man's hands doodling in the library five years ago and now recognized their cruelty. She didn't understand her time spent with the Agua Dulce man. They both suffocated her. What little room remained for her was cramped and shabby.

July. A slowly improving business hadn't mattered. Steven fought the mesquite now, added it to his list of unfinished jobs; accelerated his anxiety. He poisoned the brush, piled it up and burned it. She offered to help but he laughed, his clothes wet with sweat.

And behind that offer and laugh, his work with the ax, the barn's paint job that stayed the same, the perfect summer sky, there was the thought that drummed but didn't become monotonous or repetitious.

The Agua Dulce man suddenly grew monstrous to her. She finally batted his penis away, turned on the bed and screamed at him, found anger that amazed her but carried her on its crest until she had literally driven him out of the house. A few minutes later she heard the grate of the gears and the low whine of the truck as it descended their hill.

He continued to deliver water but Susan wasn't there. The first time, she parked the car and came around to find yellow-white pearls of semen deposited neatly atop the red plastic that plugged the bottles. The next week he pissed all over the jugs. By the month's end they stood in the small shade of the porch unviolated and cool to her palms as she lifted them onto her bruised shoulders.

Near the fourth Steven stuck a steak knife into the table top and the steady drum of the thought quickened.

Now when he left in the morning she did too. At first she drove to specific places and did specific things—errands she'd printed in block letters on the notepads headed Cameron Ag Chemicals. Before she jotted down lists for Sears or Wal-Mart or Kroger she meticulously blacked his name out and left only the address and phone numbers. Their home phone, on the right of the page, was wrong and someone had gone through the entire pad and altered each page by hand. She imagined Phil Burke, with little to sell or demonstrate, painstakingly making the changes.

She drove, did her business, and drove again across town in the heat, the windows down, the air at stop signs or traffic lights heavy and whirring with cicadas and grasshoppers.

Watering was restricted in town. Trees dropped yellow and orange leaves as if it were fall.

She drove on and ignored the drum of the thought. Without the Agua Dulce man she felt cut loose from everything. She tried to locate herself among actions: Susan picking up the cumbersome water bottles; Susan buying a dress; Susan filling the car with gas.

She drove to the empty riverbed that marked the Blanco County line. Thirty-five miles ahead was Austin, but she never went that far. Once Steven had surprised her by telling her how many miles she'd driven that Tuesday. But after the announcement he'd seemed suddenly unconcerned.

She watched his hands; they were the hands of an old man.

"We have to do something about you, you know. Something about your problem." She put down the aluminum mixing bowl and sat across the table from him. "When it comes on, can't you feel it?"

Steven folded the paper he'd jotted the mileage down on. "Sometimes I can. It's like a gentle pressure." He creased the paper with his thumb. "But sometimes it's out before I can reach it. . . I can't move quick enough. . . it's awfully fast."

Later, when she'd mentioned it again, he'd held her down in bed. He'd pinned her with his knee in the middle of her back until she grew absolutely still.

Susan came to the bridge. She pulled below it to where the fishermen launched their jonboats during the fall and spring.

She drove to the county dump. She watched the piles of trash burn, the smell cloaking the car; large black flakes of burned paper floated onto the dash. She felt herself the reaction to his actions. She determined, watching the bulldozer dig trenches and hurry the garbage underground like a noisy yellow insect, that she only reacted in movement and sound. Motion and talk. The priest, her mother, Phil Burke, the water man drifted uselessly past like the odor and the charred paper.

Near the end of the month at a roadside park she couldn't bear to see her face. She imagined how it looked. The crusts on her lips raked her tongue. She'd called home but her mother's voice had taken up all the time.

Susan got out of the car and walked to the fence. Beyond it the land sloped up to a crest of trees. There was no wind, and air felt precious to her face.

Last week she had seen a TV movie, a miniseries. And in it the Romans had waited for harbingers, they called them. Signs from the gods. They could be flights of birds or shooting stars.

She decided to let the signs tell her something. She didn't believe in the gods. But the Roman general hadn't either and still the signs came despite him and they were absolutely correct and by the last night he was puzzled himself. She put herself under the care of whatever was larger. She had neither faith nor hope. She was simply waiting for whatever moved beyond her own dumb acts.

August. Steven added an autumn garden to everything else. For Susan there were no signs though she looked anxiously everywhere. She pegged her life on the outdoors. She could hardly stay inside. She bent beside him, filling the warm holes with water.

September. The first cool weather swept through the state. From their porch on Friday nights they could see the stadium lights and hear, on the northerly wind, the rising and falling roar of the crowd.

Business gradually slackened and Steven spent long afternoons in the barn and garden. His abuse leveled out. It was there but more lethargic as if taking direction from the chilling air.

One night, in the middle of the month, Susan awoke to a cacophony of sounds: shouted gibberish; a dog barking far off; naked feet pounding across the porch.

"Susan! Help me!"

She threw off the quilt and hobbled on sleeping legs to the kitchen. Steven, fully dressed but barefoot, danced in front of the counter. The receiver shaking in his hand, he dragged the phone into the sink.

"What is it? What's happening?" Susan felt the light on her cheek before she looked beyond his shoulder and out the open door to see the line of fire just breaking through the seams of the tin on the barn roof.

"Here." Steven tossed the phone at her but ran out into the yard before she caught the slippery thing. It fell to the floor, its body banging the side of the steel sink.

She picked it up, dialed and spoke to the dispatcher. Calmly she gave the directions Steven had gotten from the old man's relatives. Five miles out 96; left on the Dale Road. Two point seven miles up. The old Hemphill place. Hanging up she moved to the door and through it onto the porch. The emerging fire broke glass and whittled its way out the far end of the barn.

She sat on the porch's edge and watched Steven dance beyond the ring of heat, his arms raised over his head, waving his hands like some Pentecostal full of the Holy Ghost.

Soon the volunteer firemen rushed up the lane and got to work. They had it out in fifteen minutes but stayed until almost dawn poking the rafters, prying charred planks off the ruined corner. Finally they congregated on the porch to drink coffee and Cokes and chide Steven for his carelessness at leaving a kerosene lamp burning. It's a dry old firetrap anyway, one of them said.

They laughed and chatted. From bed, she listened to Steven's high, almost shrill laugh as he came inside for more coffee. He knew several of the men from town.

Her eyes shut, the pillow over her head to close out their racket, she saw the red thread of fire along the eave and listened to the breaking glass. The heated tin had moaned as it reddened and twisted away from the nails. Susan recognized what the Romans had called a harbinger.

October. Her mind traveled in tedious circles. Where was help? she wondered. She reminded herself that he had never broken a bone. Not yet, she had to add. Not yet. Lately he seemed more calm. But that was no guarantee. What good is logic in all this mess of my life?

In her dreams she filled the empty gas cans again, as she really had. She watched herself take them down from the shelf on the back porch, pump in the gas at the Conoco station, and then push the heavy tins as far back on the shelf as she could until she'd need a stepladder or chair to reach them. Often now, at the end of the dream, before something else appeared to sweep her away, she was on tiptoe, her fingers scratching at the cool red and yellow paint of the cans.

So, when she awoke and sat up smelling the bittersweet odor of burning paper, she thought she was still in the dream but in some permutation of it she hadn't encountered before.

She heard a voice. From the half-opened doorway she saw a light blaze against the oak floor and die out just as quickly.

Susan got up and, shivering from the damp, walked out to the living room. Just inside the door, she gathered the loose gown around her.

There was light from the guardlight near the barn coming through the uncurtained windows. Steven sat in the far corner near the stereo, his back to the wall. He talked on as he wadded the newspaper and struck a match. But the damp paper only smoked, sent up a curling tail in the white light.

"Steven?" Susan walked onto the shag carpet and stood a yard away. She squatted and shook her head. "What are you doing, Steven?"

He looked up at her and nodded. Then he crumpled the paper into a tighter ball. "I can't get it to light."

Some of the paper he had shoved up under the edge of the couch. Susan saw how he'd littered the whole corner with wads of paper he'd taken from the trash. Dried coffee grounds stained the carpet. There was the smell of trash and the smell of charred paper.

Steven struck a blue-white flame and held it calmly to the paper. In the light from the match she saw the pages of a catalogue. The unnatural smiles of models, their heads back and arms held in uncomfortable positions.

"I almost managed with the barn, you know. But at the last minute I ran out. When I almost had it done. . . I ran away." His voice was steady. The match went out but not before it burned down to the flesh. "This should be easier, don't you think?"

Susan stood, her knees creaking, and looked down at her husband in his pajamas in the corner of the room.

"Can't you help? I've got to stop myself."

She crossed the room and went out the kitchen door. She kept to the gravel drive but at one point had to cross a patch of ankle-high weeds. Then she was glad it was cold and the snakes were gone.

She stopped in the lane that went down the hill to the asphalt road. Overhead the sky was bright with stars. Standing there she waited for the decision; for the outcome. She pictured herself on the road: a woman, dressed for sleep, at the edge of some woods, near a house and barn.

March. Phil Burke pulled his old pickup to the curb in front of the small brick house and moved to the passenger's side. "I could help you do that, you know."

Susan stood up from the circular flowerbed she'd been edging with heavy stone blocks. "Just a few more. I can manage."

Phil Burke smiled and slid back under the wheel. "They treating you good at the phone company?"

Susan nodded. "I like it there. It's a fine job."

He drove off and she finished the flowerbed. She waved at her neighbors across the street scurrying in under loads of groceries. At the kitchen sink she washed the dirt from her hands and face; then she opened the mail.

Taking the sales catalogues with her, she sat in the living room. The furniture still smelled new, the fabric of the couch was unwrinkled. When she stopped to think or when she remembered her dreams she saw him as the boy in the library bent over the opened texts, but instead of taking notes he doodled in long, looping spirals, the pencil's glaze cracked by his teeth.

Junior Jackson's Parable

I tore out to Mama's. Punched the old Chevy pickup and slung gravel halfway down Paper-mill Drive. I'd left the goddamned phone out in the service bay at the Firestone store dangling after the bitch'd hung up on me.

I flew past the Sonic. Luckless sonofabitch, I kept saying. Luckless, worthless, sorry stupid sonofabitch. And pushed down harder on the accelerator, rattling the shitty unleaded through the carb.

I guess I'd had enough. Roger Blake, my court-appointed lawyer, said that later a hundred times. He painted all sorts of pictures of me and her and him—mostly true—but some I couldn't quite make out. Wondered who the hell he was talking about exactly. But the fucking D.A.! What a peckerhead he was. When he called his surprise witness a couple of days before the trial ended and grinned down at me, all three of us knew I'd really fucked the duck. I dropped my stare to my ugly worthless hands.

But I didn't only have the shotgun on my mind. That's what the peckerhead kept harping on. The shotgun. Twelve-gauge. Buckshot, ladies and gentlemen of the jury. I mean, it passed through my mind, sure, but I'd had enough, you know. I guess I was mainly just going to Mama's and leaving everything behind—the Firestone store, our mobile home over in Regency Gardens behind Wal-Mart, the Casbah Club. Daddy's

25

gun came to me somewhere on the farm-to-market road. Came
and went. Came back some more. Sitting in his closet behind
boxes of coveralls he'd saved from the mill, old broken Emer-
son fans. In my mind maybe I even crammed the gun back
deeper, covered it with clothes.

Remember, you'd had enough, Roger Blake reminded me.
And he wasn't lying; I'd had all the shit a man can take. Luckless bastard.

Mr. Stroud had yelled from the front of the Firestone store,
over some cutouts of Richard Petty. The two women customers
behind him and to his left open-mouthed. Ed, the other under-
paid employee, standing up under a car on the rack as I skid-
ded past, burning rubber. His eyes bugged out. Where I have
a limp, he has a twisted, smaller-than-a-twig right forearm.
He tucks tools in the bony crook. Together we hobble, gimp
around the place. That story another example of my luck.
Up under a car at Walker's Sinclair over by the tracks when
I was just sixteen and the jack decides to let down. Simply
spews out fluid in a long spurt and drops the fucking Buick
across my shin. Sixteen and the makings of a gimp. Some quack
at the county hospital working by the hour patched me up.
A couple of okay years and then it starts hurting like a bastard
right after I get in the Navy.

I'm driving past the road to the dump, gimpy leg aching,
and I reach down to rub it. What do you think it all means?
I'm asking. First I keep reeling it around over and over. Then
I blurt it out to the noisy Chevy cab—coffee cups rattling,
cigarette packs slithering from side to side on the dash. But
I don't even smoke. I don't take the time to light up. Now
that shows you the state I'm in.

"Why that day? That particular time?" Roger Blake asked
me on the stand. But I don't know. I'd had enough bad luck.
But I didn't mention luck. I kept that to myself. "You'd been
married a little over two years?" "Yes sir." "She'd been Bud

Frazer's girlfriend before your marriage?" "Yes sir." Marriage, I'd thought. Shit on that.

"Hey, come on by for a beer when you get off, okay?" she'd said as soon as I'd answered the phone. I'd tucked the greasy receiver under my chin.

Ed had scuttled past, edged by me, his little arm clenching a ratchet and some extensions. Me and Mary Louise had been up late the night before fighting. She'd been high on something. Some pills he'd gotten her. She'd come in at three. But just a week before, she'd sworn no later than nine or ten from now on. Just a few free hours, she'd said, after she finished work at the Catfish Castle. Free hours, she called them. Shit on that too.

"You're takin' those pills again! Don't lie to me, Mary Louise." I raised my voice and Ed looked away, scampered back up under the Cougar; he was used to all this. "Goddammit, you promised you'd stop. You said you'd leave him alone!" I swallowed to stifle a whine.

The house was always a mess. We'd argue and then drink. Bud would drop by to talk. He was from South Carolina and he'd served time for murder and assault and other shit. Mary Louise told me about his tattoos once. Even about the one on his dick—a dozen arrows that swelled into rockets. She'd laughed and snuggled up to me and said she was all mine now but those tattoos of his are hilarious. Are, I kept thinking. She'd said *are*.

The prosecution wanted to take out the part about the arrows but the judge decided not to. Twenty-four eyes batted when Roger Blake said *penis* over and over.

"Hey, boy." She'd given Bud the phone or he'd taken it. I heard her laughing in the background. Some band was warming up at the Casbah Club.

"Come on by and I'll buy you a couple. We're havin' a fine time already."

"Sounds like it."

"Huh?"

"I thought you were going to leave her alone."

He was big and moved like a bear or one of them sloths at the zoo. He went to sheriff department picnics. He drove a truck for Gulf Freight Lines. And he scared everybody shitless.

"Come on by and we'll party. Come on."

"You said you'd leave her alone. You said you would."

The band tuned up some more and Mary Louise buzzed something into the receiver. Bud laughed right into it for a minute. Then I listened to the band playing "Blue Eyes Crying in the Rain" out of key and awful-sounding on the phone.

"Suit yourself, you little motherfucker."

"Let me talk to her, Bud. Put her on."

"Oh, Bud," she laughed, and then, "Come on, you old asshole. We'll have a good time. Bud'll buy."

Remember all them examples in church? I'd come into Big Church, as Mama called it, from Sunday School and there were these stories the preacher'd tell. The very same plane this guy missed crashed not ten minutes after he'd missed it. Somebody'd gone from whiskey to heroin, his life on the skids. But one afternoon, as he'd laid dirty and lonely and sick on an overdose, he'd watched a trail of ants on the floor. Helping share the burden of a breadcrumb. And he'd seen his own need for other people's help.

Everybody always understood something. Everything fit together and made sense at the end. Explained the car wreck, the alcoholic's whipping his wife, the sparrow falling from the sky. That and them parables. The Good Samaritan finally helped that hurt guy; the prodigal son's daddy fixed a feast for him. Everything sorted itself out. A whole lifetime of sin, uselessness, bad luck was cleared up, explained, paid for, worked out in a minute flat.

A man came to sing once. His face eaten totally away

by acid from an exploding battery. Not till that explosion had he really valued life. And later, faceless, he'd praised God for the moment of revelation. He'd warbled out "Oh, why not tonight?", his skin plastic and tight.

"Mary Louise, you leave there right now. You hear me?"

"But Bud brought me."

"Don't argue, dammit! You get someone else to take you home. You promised. . ."

She hung up. Or Bud did. She testified he did. But who knows about that? She's back heavy into drugs already. And I got a letter from her lawyer yesterday talking about divorce, getting the mobile home and everything else. Sure, why not? *What* everything else?

I sort of lied. What else could I do? I said I was in a blind rage. Yeah, he'd been tearing my home apart. Yeah, he'd been supplying my wife with drugs. Yeah, I did suspect they'd been having sex. Shit, she soaked her underwear every night in the kitchen sink. I smelled him on her skin. Yeah, yeah, yeah, I was afraid of him. That's the whole truth there. He was a scary fucker. Solid. Big. Tattooed. Somehow friends of the cops. Dangerous. Fill in the blank about him. And only use bad words.

But it wasn't blind rage. It was too jumbled up for just that simple answer. But I knew the peckerhead wanted the maximum he could get—thirty years, or so Roger Blake had said. I knew I had to play up the passionate rage part, leave out the stuff about bad luck.

I drove up to Mama's gate and turned off the engine. I caught my breath for the first time. But I didn't leap out and up the steps. Nope. I settled back and shook out a Winston and lit it and sucked it deep.

Junior Jackson. That's me. Junior luckless, meaningless Jackson. Crippled by a falling car. What'd Mama used to say. . .? "Jun'er, don't hold them magazines over your eyes to read, somethin'll drop out and blind you . . . stick right in your eyeball." Good start, huh? "Don't lean back in the chair, Jun'er, it'll break and ram a piece up your spine. Damaged for life."

Oh sure, blame your mama and daddy, right? But how about the old man? Fell off a log truck at thirty, crushed a shoulder, spends the rest of his life in a little pain, sitting in front of the TV in his vinyl lounger saying "It's ever' dog eat a dog out there." "The world's a fucking mess, Jun'er." And later even more fuel. "What's that shit about them Arabs and Jews?" Arabs and Jews. Nigras on the dole. Mama'd hobble in, her knees locked from arthritis—Arthur, Daddy called it— and they'd shake their heads over TV (when I was little it had been the radio; neither could read much). And when things got real bad they'd both sleep. Take to their beds if the car broke down, the well pump needed new packing, something had eaten her pullets. Living at home, I'd do the same. Until finally, after twelve, fourteen hours of silence with only the faucets dripping, the wind blowing across the eaves, one of us would crawl out of bed, make a pot of coffee, force his thoughts on the problem, wake the others up.

The first year with Mary Louise, I slept most of the weekends until I decided I might ought to go out with her and try keeping up.

They met me at the back door; Wolf, the old black-and-tan, as slow as Mama.

"Surgery's the only thing, the doctor says. They'll cut along here," she bends gingerly to slide a finger over her kneecap, "and lift it out. Put in a plastic one."

"Plastic. . . shee-it." Daddy's leaning over the table pecking at a bought apple pie they've picked to pieces.

"He was a wild man," Mama said on the stand. I didn't look at her then or later. The old man broke down in tears. I think he thought he was on trial for something himself. The Jews, Arabs, nigras had finally finagled him out of his lounger to humiliate him.

"Want some pie?" she'd asked.

Somewhere along the way it had dawned on me that maybe all this would become the moment of revelation like the ends of those parables. Do all this in order to get to the sense of things.

Hmmm, I thought. And went in to take the shotgun, check the shells, walk straight through the house to the front door.

That's sort of how I went in the Navy. Then the god-damned leg gets worse and worse from all that marching and exercise and fighting them practice oil fires. So this Navy doctor says it'll be fine and dandy after he opens it up and unpinches something and rotates something else. Shit, I don't believe in doctors like Mama and I'm already homesick, so I'm out of there in a minute. All the way to Quartzite, Arizona, before they pick me up AWOL. Of course they didn't just give me a medical. The monkey-suited bastards process me out with a D.D. Junior Jackson, D.D. So I finally did get to come home to work at Beasley's Shell station, though it was a pretty crooked route.

The peckerhead brought up my run-ins with the law. But it was just the usual kid stuff and I'd never served any time for it. Just warnings and a couple of J.P. fines. Stealing a couple of tires, a tape player—that sort of thing. We'd drink, go to the high school games in town, drink some more and smoke some dope. End up smashing a window and taking tapes, radios, fuzzbusters. Everybody did it. It was more a sport—like hunting deer out of season—than something bad. We stole from each other most of the time.

But I quit it. When I got the job changing flats and mounting tires at the Firestone place, I went cold turkey. Some of the guys said me and Ed was sitting on top a gold mine, but I said no. Besides, I was the one who always got caught—figures—and this job was my only way to stay out of jail.

"She's trouble," Daddy'd said, his head level with his toes, looking between them at "Gunsmoke."

Mama'd shook her head as Mary Louise'd drove off in her Camaro after her first visit.

It'd turn out bad. Trouble. Misery. Out of luck. First the Navy business and a dishonorable discharge. Then coming back to steal. What'd we teach you anyway? Then they'd troop to bed to recharge their last sparks into a smolder.

They were right. I was right, too—I'd thought the same thing when I saw her first inhale dope for a new world's record. Saw the first boyfriend, Bud, she'd had since moving down from Norman.

But when she opened those long, brown legs what can I say? Nobody asked about that at the trial.

"He was like a wild animal I'm tellin' you. All tussled hair, eyes wild, bugged out."

"I don't know. I can't rightly say," the old man kept saying. They must have done some Olympic sleeping the first couple of weeks. I know I did. They'd take me back up—who the fuck did I know who'd make bail?—and the nigras would catcall, thump burning butts at me, jeer. And I'd lay down and sleep and dream luckless dreams. A vacuum that sucked the hours up, shortened my life without refreshing me one bit.

All the shit at the Casbah's a mess. It wasn't like the movies. Not in regular motion or slow motion like them Peckinpah flicks. It was in fast motion; more like old Keystone Kop movies or WWI where doughboys scurry past, their legs pumping nine to nothing.

I sat and cried most of the first week of the trial. I was shocked by what had happened at the club. And it was so fast it could replay itself in my head fifty times a minute.

So I thought it over and over while the peckerhead D.A. trotted out everything about my life he could find. The theft charges they'd dropped; Mary Louise's drug problem. Her and Bud. Poor old Bud Frazer, he'd say, a victim of us sorry white trash—that's what he'd meant, anyway. And I'd think about it and couldn't help crying. But not for Bud, you see. Fuck him. Though I was sorry about it all and pretty damned confused. I was crying for Mary Louise, who I glanced at now and then, who sat blank-eyed resting her clean shiny brown hair against the oak paneling. And I cried about my bad luck.

Toward the end of the week, Roger Blake began putting on people who knew Bud; people from South Carolina even, and they had some stories to tell. Bad-assed wasn't the half of it.

"You'd seen him at the Casbah Club before?"

Old decrepit Mickey Cotter'd drank with us a hundred nights there. "Yes sir."

"How'd he act in there? How'd he treat people?"

"Shit!"

The judge leaned over quickly and spoke to Cotter.

"Sorry, your honor." He scratched his fuzzy chin and talked on.

I replayed the scene.

All the way back into town I'd argued with myself like them angels sitting on your shoulder—the good one and the bad one.

Way back in my mind I kept thinking that this would end it all somehow. I'd take her home, wash her face with a cold washrag like I'd done before, and put her to bed. Maybe I'd pull up her t-shirt and run a finger over her wide pink nipples.

The twelve-gauge shotgun bounced on the seat but I only heard it. I didn't look at it at all. It was really for protection. Just in case, that's all. I sweated and the air rushing in the rolled-down window only made me stickier. Dried in a film on my greasy face. I smelled myself, my body odor strong from the day's work. But stronger than that by now.

But all this went fast as I rolled up in the parking lot at dusk, jumped out, went in and sat down at their table, ordered a beer and looked away for a time before I jerked my head around and told Bud to take his arm from her neck, the fingers of his left hand—crowded with nugget rings—squeezing her tight nipple. Houston Oilers, the t-shirt said, and I stared at the message.

Objections would interrupt me a little, you know. The peckerhead kept harping about me going all the way to Mama's to get the gun. He wanted thirty years at least, Roger Blake kept saying. But my witnesses just talked about Bud. Someone said you'd need a couple of shotguns for him. You couldn't find a single friend. None of his sheriff buddies talked. Homewrecker, ruined lives, tattooed penis, belligerent.

Belligerent, shit. I'd wipe my eyes, glance at Mary Louise who sat staring straight at the space just over the white-faced clock. Here like the TV shows. Perry Mason. Except this was less real. Everything seemed too soft. The tabletop gave a little. I sank too deep into the oak chair. The paper tissue the hardest surface anywhere around.

"Oh, I seen him do awful things to people at the bar. Cuss 'em. Taunt 'em. Shove 'em around like he owned the place. Beat the. . .hell out of 'em in the parking lot."

There were cars parked every which way as usual. I towed her through the door. She seemed dead weight, like dragging something that weighed a lot more than it looked. I shoved her in the pickup but going around to my door I stopped.

Bud moved like a bear from the door of his den to a car right in front of my Chevy. He grinned, rested a huge hip on the rear fender. The sheet metal dipped in.

"Let her out now, Jun'er. Be a good boy and let her come out to play with old Buddy boy. Okay, Jun'er?"

And this all quick motion too, sped up, the film sprockets rattling like mad, the machine clattering. I'm terrified, smell myself suddenly, but I'm all scrambled up with the need to do something final to free us for the feast, the happy ending. Something that makes good sense.

I jerked the gun out from under Mary Louise and through the window. I had come to kill him. The frames snapping faster, breakneck speed.

He cussed me, sitting idly on the fender. Then in his bear's movement he lifted his hip off. Turned to see the people gathered at the door. I looked to see them all open-mouthed. A few took quick swallows of beer. The silver cans caught the parking lot lights.

I said something. Bud moved like a wall, or train, gliding easily toward me, his left hand out. Everything quick and full of things at the same time. Mary Louise blew the horn, held it down until minutes after I'd aimed for his head and then, finally, shot at his legs, the dust coming up to tangle with his shredded khaki pants. I saw how I'd riddled the car's fender. A tire hissed. Mary Louise let up on the horn and the people in front of the bar took a couple of steps and stopped again.

I couldn't look at his face. I couldn't kill him. I didn't even pump in another shell. All I could think of was how much I hoped this ended it all. Though it didn't seem much of an ending to anything important.

When Mary Louise screamed I stared in the dark window in surprise. Her finger jabbed at the windshield and I looked at Bud for the first time just to see him cough and spit in my direction and fall, bounce off my hood, land like a boulder in the floating dust. The single ricocheted pellet. Off the bumper and up through his left temple.

There were color slides. The peckerhead brought them. The bailiff set up the projector and screen. The shiny pointer circled the stuff like chewed newspaper that had dribbled from his head onto the hospital sheet. And I cried.

I lied too. I'd gone to kill him, not just scare him, and I'd chickened out. Junior Jackson, the chickenshit sonofabitch who'd shot at the ground and missed. He'd got two superficial leg wounds, but one of the pellets had come up off the bumper and into his brain. Off the heavy chrome bumper of a blue and white '57 Ford. Everything since made from shitty metal or plastic. But let's talk luck, huh? That's why I cried. Slept in the cell as if I'd died too. Mary Louise didn't come by. I asked Roger Blake to talk to her for me. The D.A. wanted thirty fucking years. All I wanted was them to brick up the rusty bars and window and let me sleep. In my luckless dreams the shooting expanded so I could try to cram meaning in a thousand pockets of air where nothing happened. In the pickup. At Daddy's closet door. Between the gun barrel and Mary Louise's ass. Unlucky stupid bastard. I think only Bud came out prepared. I'm fucked up. Fucked over. She's stoned shit-less. Bud's the man with his hand out, sliding along the fender. The dented metal popping out without a sound.

But this is the part that lays me out like you'd smacked me with a shovel.

About six days into the trial I'd cried myself pretty dry. After a shitty breakfast and kicking the huge water roaches I'd smashed that night into a pile, I'd change into the blue seer-sucker Roger Blake had brought me and they'd lead me down. I'd sit but not listen now, the courtroom breezeless, the suit hot, sweat dripping down the small of my back. They put everybody on: the police, the coroner with his lousy slides, everybody else in the Casbah parking lot. Mary Louise, me, the whole nine yards.

But Wednesday afternoon after a supper of hash browns and those link sausages Daddy called donkey dicks, I stretched out, used to the loud racket of the place. Nigras bullshitting one another with a vengeance. Cell doors clanging. The pile of roaches still there and big enough to give you the creeps.

Then Blake shows up and sits on the cot with me. He opens his fat battered briefcase full of legal pads and folders and rolls of Lifesavers and offers me a wintergreen and sits back, his hands across his stomach.

Mostly I'm numb by now. I think that's why the noise doesn't bother me anymore. Four weeks in here and I'm numb like a catfish you'd thumped on the head. Waiting for the cold knife up the asshole.

But Blake fidgets and shifts away from the light through my window and edges close to me, his breath a burst of mint the smell of Pepto-Bismol. He's a good man, I've decided. But the busted veins that start on his nose and flare out across his cheeks say he's got problems, too. I don't think he's any too lucky either and that figures in like everything else.

But he whispers something and reaches out to give my knee a tremendous whack and squeeze and then he bellylaughs and I have to sit up closer to get his drift. He talks on now, fumbling through the briefcase, but instead of another mint, he takes out some folders.

"Just be quiet about it. Keep your head down in there a few more days. It's looking real fine." And he goes on and on, fidgeting with happiness.

After he leaves I lay down in a state. "You haven't been listening, paying good attention, looking at the jury like I have, that's all. I didn't want to say anything sooner though I noticed it after the business about the penis. Didn't want to get your hopes up too much." And he'd whacked me again a couple of times. "We'll walk on this. Bud Frazer was a sorry bastard. It was almost a community service. Him a snitch for the sheriff, too. Some protection there. I'd guess five years probated. Probated, Junior." He'd whacked me again, leaned back and crossed his arms over his stomach.

I'll walk, I keep saying over and over. And toward morning—the moon flying across my high small window—I nodded and stood up for the millionth time. Goddammit, maybe it was all going to work out. I'd shot him by accident and that'll walk me out of here and with that bastard gone me and Mary Louise'll do fine. Now I'd feel the kick of the gun and hear the splatter of pellets against the fender and dirt but I'd shrug it off. God works in mysterious ways, Mama'd say.

I paced. Then I'd lay down. I felt light-headed, the man in the story, my stupid fucking life making some sense. If I'd shot the fucker down, they'd toss me in the pen for thirty years. But I had cried real tears too, and pity and mercy and all that stuff was being leveled at me, Junior Jackson. Junior Jackson, not guilty or maybe guilty but probated. He was sure and by full daybreak so was I.

It was a miracle. I ain't no Pentecostal like Mama but that morning I almost shook with the Holy Ghost and spoke in tongues.

The trial was almost over. Maybe another three days. But that Thursday I didn't care about anything. I listened more and saw how right he was. The jurors looked kind and sym-pathetic. I could see all this had been hard on them too. Once I started doodling on a spare yellow pad but like a hawk Blake's hand swept over and took the pen away. I'd written my name down one side and next to it Mary Louise Jackson. I'd glanced around at her in the corner. All that dope didn't do much for her wanting sex, but after seeing her there, her hair shiny and long, the light brown of acorns, my dick nudged the hell out of the seersucker.

After supper I listened to the bullshit. I reached around the wall of my cell and took a Kool from the guy next door. Willy'd been in about two weeks charged with car theft. We knew some guys in common, so we talked all sorts of shit. He smoked my Winstons and I smoked his Kools.

Almost dark Friday night, they took me down to their dirty little reception room where I'd gone to talk to Mama a couple of times.

Friday had looked even better for me. By Tuesday it could all be over, Roger Blake had said. I smiled at the fat fucker of a guard. He stood by the door and inhaled Pall Malls, gabbed to himself, waved his cigarette.

Mary Louise slumped at the filthy cheap table, her hair hiding most of her face.

My face lit up and I reached across the table to take her hands. This time my pecker rubbed rough twill.

"Hey, you okay?"

She looked up and nodded. Her eyes were flat as slate. Like looking into a blackboard for some emotions. She was high. It was in the slope of her shoulders too, and the way her head lolled a bit too loose.

"Shit, Mary Louise, you're fucked up. I thought you were staying at Mama's?"

She nodded. Her hands under mine were ice-cold, the coldest thing I'd touched in weeks.

But I was too happy to let her get me down for long. So I squeezed her hands, ran my forefinger up and down her palm. My zipper close to busting.

"Roger Blake says I can walk on this. He told you that, didn't he?" She nodded. Mumbled something. "Honey, I love you, you know that. I only wanted us together. With him gone we'll have a good chance now. Hell, we'll move to Norman or somewhere. Houston's booming, they say. Okay? I'll borrow some money and rent my own station. Shit, I'll sell a million tires. I'm good at that. Okay?"

And on I went until the guard had a pile of butts to match my cockroaches and he slung himself over to cough out a "Let's go, asshole."

I stopped at the door and watched her stand and look at me and then she grinned like she used to when we'd go to a high school game together and yell till we were hoarse.

I almost leapt up the cement steps, gimpy leg and all, and swung the door shut behind me. If I'd believed a lot in God, like Mama, I'd have got on my knees. Then again, I thought about how everybody really does believe. They have to, specially when things start going right. So maybe I mumbled something and went to the wall to jerk a thumb up to

Willy Devereaux, the car thief. He passed over a Kool and I traded him a Winston. And we hung our hands out and inhaled deep as we could and blew smoke towards the bull-shitting nigras.

His old lady'd come by with some cookies. They were store-bought but we ate a dozen apiece. And I told him about seeing Mary Louise and how we'd move to Norman. He said he knew of a closed Conoco station in town, out past the loop. We wondered about the rent.

"But you'll have to put all that good stuff off, huh?"

"Not a bit."

"Shee-it, man, you're gonna do some ser'us time in them Walls."

I took a deep breath and blew puffs of Kool toward the babbling nigras. "My lawyer's gonna walk me right out of here. And then I'll open up that station. Batteries, tires — look at the price of gas. Hell, station owners must be putting back a fortune." And we talked on. He shook my hand a couple of times. Told me he could use a job someday, knew a hell of a lot about cars. "I'll bet," I said. And we laughed and later I laid down but didn't sleep. Instead I jerked off twice, one right after the other, while trying to forget Mary Louise's cold hands.

I'm Junior Jackson, remember? Remember me? So you can guess the rest.

Sure enough. Monday morning bright and early the peck-erhead brings Willy Devereaux out dressed in a lime-green seer-sucker suit. I guess maybe lawyers have some sort of deal at Weiner's. And Roger Blake looks at me sharply, his veins like black ink lines across his face, and I just stare at him and then back at Willy.

Willy lies like a sonofabitch of course. Has me strutting and cocky, a stone-cold murderer. The court buzzes, the old blue-haired ladies in the audience whispering hard. Blake objects and objects but the judge makes him sit down. Later Blake tears into Willy about the deal he'd struck with the D.A. All that sort of shit. But when he comes back and sits in the oak chair, he doesn't look at me at all. Instead he takes a roll of Lifesavers from his shirt pocket and bites off one end.

And I don't look up at the jury because I know they're staring at me with jaws locked tight, fingers squeezing each other. I don't look at Mary Louise because I'm afraid she's just looking at the clock. Instead I look straight ahead at a spot about a foot under the short flagpole the American flag's on. There's a crack in the plaster and it looks like a river from up in a plane. A river cutting through snow. I let it carry Junior Jackson off because it's pretty fucking plain to see that this story don't end like old Job getting a bunch of new sheep and camels, a wife and kids. Or with the prodigal son's homecoming feast. Or even old Jonah spit up on the beach with a new line of work.

I've been here six months. Roger Blake says I'll only serve three years max. "It could have been a lot worse," he says. He don't need to mention it could have been a whole lot better.

Here's what I've learned so far: You call nigras blacks; you can make a mean shiv out of a sharpened tablespoon; if you drop the soap in the showers, don't bend down to pick it up.

Now there's some revelations to take to the bank. There's the lessons. Maybe when I get out I'll make my living going from revival to revival. I'll stand up at the pulpit and give the bastards my story. At the end I'll raise my arms high over my head, my face sweating, and deliver the meaning of it all. Won't it be fine to see their faces before the organ starts up.

Breaking and Entering

THE glossy photographs were tucked neatly in the briefcase at Paul's side. That morning, when they were first passed to him, he had quickly turned them toward the light so the glare would obliterate most of their madness. Now, as he drove toward home, he tried not to think about them. Instead he thought about the beach house in Crystal City he and Nancy had talked about buying. How badly he needed the soothing calm of the coast. If only he could go there now, escape from the photographs and the explanations to the newspapers and all the rest of it...

As he turned recklessly into his driveway, his mind on Crystal City, the heavy bumper of the New Yorker shuddered against the gatepost. Paul winced as the wood splintered and the huge car, forced by the broken root of the post, slipped off the concrete driveway and sank a neat trench through the late-blooming mums.

Angrily he yanked the wheel, and the whining power steering pulled the car crossways, the grill coming to rest in the hedge under the children's bedroom window.

"Goddamn it to hell." Paul pounded on the padded steering wheel with his damp palms. But he refused to look at the damage. It'll wait, he told himself. And with a loping step he skirted the sideways car and ran up the steps.

Paul wanted to avoid Nancy, but the front door opened onto a long hallway and she stood at the far end in the kitchen,

43

her profile toward him, her small, tightly packed body in a bikini with his chef's apron over it. She tore at a head of lettuce. On the tile counter near her wooden salad bowl were scattered tomatoes. At this distance and in the muted light of early afternoon, they shone like splotches of blood.

Carefully he closed the door but so intently had he been watching her in his anxiety to escape unnoticed that she seemed to sense his gaze and looked around with a shudder.

"Oh, Paul!" She dropped the lettuce into the bowl. Her hand brushed against the tomatoes and several skittered to the floor.

"Hello." Paul waved with a flick of his wrist and, as Nancy bent to pick up the scattered vegetables, he trotted down the hall to the bathroom. With the door closed he crossed to the lavatory and spun the taps to full force. Their angry sputter reminded him of his promised repair—this, like other chores, methodically outlined on the refrigerator door, stuck there with small magnets in the shapes of crayons and miniature potholders and bunches of grapes. Next to his list was hers and under theirs, the children's. It was an orderly arrangement, a system that worked, that they were all happy with.

He took off his trousers, laid them neatly over a towel rack, and sat on the toilet to let the pain in his bowels, the ache that had been there for hours—through the long series of meetings instigated by the photos and the news they brought—twist and cramp his intestines. The sweat collected on his forehead. Through the partially raised window he could hear the distant splash of his children in their backyard pool.

"Paul?" Nancy pecked at the door. "What's wrong? You're home an hour early."

His hand brushed the briefcase that leaned against the tub.

"Paul?" She rapped again.

"Nancy." His voice was rough and instantly he was sorry. "Nancy, it's nothing. Just a touch of diarrhea."

"Oh."

He could picture her with a forefinger on her cheek, her lips pursed and twisted to the left as she thought.

"I'll get the Kaopectate out of Judith's room. It'll do the trick."

"In a minute." The twisting rumble under his navel made him grimace. "I'll be fine in just a minute."

"Nonsense," she said, her tone the one she used on recalcitrant children.

After a few minutes, when the pain had dimmed, Paul moved his hand across to the rough leather of the case. The sharp click of the latches echoed off the tile.

The light entering the small window was filtered through the leaves of the huge live oak outside near the garage. So, as he arranged the pictures cautiously on the rim of the tub across from the toilet, they took on a green tint. Where the glare of the harsh fluorescent lights had aided him in his office, here the dull underwater light took some of the edge off. But not enough.

Mr. Shaw lay near the front door, his pajama bottoms wet with blood to the knees. The flap was open, the flaccid penis dark pink against the white cotton. His head lay over one end of the metal grating of a floor furnace. What sort of impact did it take, the FBI agents had wondered, to force the skull so far down into the metal?

Mrs. Shaw was in the kitchen. The three children were scattered in between. The oldest daughter had been stuffed into the narrow space between the washer and dryer. It was early last night, Thursday night, when her date had found them all.

Paul reached out, brought his hand up from his sore gut and touched the photograph of the youngest, the only boy. Some Legos protruded from under the body. Frozen in the policeman's flash were two posters: the ominous helmeted head of Darth Vader and the anorexic beauty of Charlie's Angels.

"Hey, you still in there? Here's the medicine." Nancy turned the handle. "Paul, you've locked the door." She rattled it in frustration. "Paul, answer me."

"I'm better. Just fine now, as a matter of fact." He cocked his head to the side at the sound of his weak voice. "Be out in a few minutes. Think I'll shower." He sat anxiously on the edge of the sweaty seat until she left.

Slowly he gathered the pictures and placed them in their manila folders. Then he stood and began stripping off his shirt and tie. It's not your fault, they'd told him. Anderson, the agent in charge, had patted him on the shoulder and smiled.

No, it's really not, Paul told himself and turned to look in the mirror. He turned off the roaring taps and listened to the few final drops fall in the basin.

He knew he was a good lawyer. A fine tax lawyer and hell with contracts and leases. And quite a politician — they all said that. For a moment he smiled and then he reached down for the case and stood naked in the green light.

No one could have known it would happen, Anderson had said. You try to sense everything but you're not always going to bat a thousand. Not forever.

As United States Attorney for three years, he'd never personally tried a case. Oversaw them all, sure, but left the details to his assistants. He was excellent at delegating authority.

It's one of those things, Anderson had said, lighting a cigarette. Paul could almost smell the harsh odor now. He had been amazed at the steadiness of the agent's hand.

But Paul had helped get Cox, the murderer, into the Federal Witness Protection Program over a year ago after he had agreed to testify against some of his cronies who ran an interstate extortion ring based in Austin. In return, they'd gotten some aggravated assault charges against him dropped. Sure he was violent, Paul thought. His record showed that clearly enough. But not crazy. And Paul's assistants, the agents, everyone had assured him of the necessity of Cox's testimony. Cox had probably only seen the Shaws once or twice since he'd moved a block down the street from them. Paul shook his head slowly. Still, it was his name, Paul Winslow, scrawled leisurely across the bottom of the government forms.

Paul stood in front of the mirror, his head light, his naked feet sticking to the damp tile floor. Political appointment, the newspapers had called it. Well, weren't they all? He nodded at himself in the mirror.

The children splashed and screamed outside and Nancy whistled along with the radio as Paul showered furiously.

Later, after he had dressed, Paul locked his briefcase, shoved it as far up under his desk as he could, and came out to sit next to Nancy on the screened-in porch that overlooked their pool and backyard. The children, their numbers increased by six or eight friends and neighbors, seethed like a hive.

"Need this?" Nancy asked and picked the plastic bottle of medicine off a low table.

Paul slumped in the vinyl webbing and rubbed his tired eyes. "No, I'm okay now."

"I saw the car and the fence." Nancy reached across to stroke his thigh. "What's the matter?"

Paul looked straight ahead at the pool and stopped her hand by covering it with his own. "Some problems downtown. Some reorganizing going on. Justice wants me to step up some white-collar crime investigations. It'll make county officials mad as hell." He wasn't lying or inventing any of this. It was really happening, although smoothly, without a hitch. "I'm sorry about the flowers. And they were doing so well despite this heat."

Nancy shrugged and smiled. "I'll call the insurance company about the fence and fender. The flowers you and I can replant. You with such a knack for landscaping." She stood and stretched, still wearing her bikini. Paul noticed the three-inch scar over her spine, midway down her back. It was from surgery for a slipped disc. He marveled at how long ago that had all been. Like another life really, he thought.

She waved at the children and turned to go. "Want a drink?" she asked over her shoulder.

"Listen. Sit for a minute."

Nancy pursed her lips and twisted them to one side as she leaned against the door.

"I'd like to get away from all that bullshit downtown for a while. You know, let the rest of them sort it out themselves. Anderson said"— and for a split second his thoughts crowded together all the agent had really said during the last few hours—"he said nothing was going to break soon anyway." Paul shifted uncomfortably in the chair. "So, what if I drive down to Crystal City and look at that beach house Lynne told us about?"

Nancy straightened and reached over to give Paul a strong hug. Laughing, he shrugged it off. "What do you think?"

"You know damned well what I've thought for months. Wonderful!" She raised her hands over her head and pirouetted awkwardly on the concrete. "Marvelous! I'll go call Lynne and get the realtor's name." She danced out of the room and left Paul with only the noisy children clustered around the diving board at the far end of the pool, their shouts mixed with the nervous bark of a distant dog.

"Wasn't it a strange name?" he spoke over his shoulder. "Like Bo or Ho or Mo?" But Nancy had already passed into the sprawling house.

In his youth Crystal City had seemed like paradise. Then there had been a ferry run by the highway department instead of the huge dramatic hump of the causeway. And his father, the smoke from his pipe brushed flat by the steady breeze, would hold him up from the observation deck and turn him to all the sights—the burned brittle hull of a World War I troopship; the gas flares from the dozens of oil wells; the gulls at the stern begging crackers; porpoises roiling in the oily wake of the ferry.

Paul slowed the car and switched off the air conditioner. On the other side of the bridge, the island flattened into the precise symmetrical lines he loved so. Hurricane Carla had destroyed much of the old beauty, and he almost stopped once or twice on the outskirts of the small central town of two or three thousand. The grand houses were utterly gone. The gentle southern concave curve of the bay that had sheltered the single row of gulf-facing mansions was a riot of broken pilings and kudzu that topped every tree and bush with a tangled conformity. Often all that remained were broad steps littered with the coruscating grit of broken glass.

He had seen the news pictures years ago, of course. But he had no idea the damage had been so tremendous. The ferry had been a portion of his childhood, a memory he loved in part because it had vanished.

The sea breeze blurred the windshield with salt as he swung the car sharply toward the white glare of the town.

And here too he shook his head in disbelief. This side of town he remembered well because here, docked immediately behind the stolid pastel faces of the fishermen's houses, were hundreds of shrimpers and beached dinghies, all the paraphernalia of the sea. Here the gulls flew in and out of the gables and landed on the low stone walls topped with shells and bits of broken colored glass. But now these houses were left to the bitter sea air and the pastels were gone, the wood bare and soft and pitted. The streets were littered with trash—a pile of soiled disposable diapers against a step; sidewalks paved with flattened tin cans. Behind the houses only an occasional fishing boat in terrible disrepair swayed lethargically in its moorings.

And in every doorway he detected the lustrous eyes of Oriental children. Their black hair glistened against the duller darkness behind them as gulls dipped and rose near the eaves.

He stepped on the accelerator, stirring up the flotsam in the street, then loosened his tie and mopped his forehead with a wad of tissue from the glove box. Some of the houses he sped past looked burned out with precision.

He rolled up the window and turned the air conditioner on full blast. Quickly the coolness dried the irritating patches of sweat on his stomach. He remembered that there had been trouble with some boat people relocated here. They had been too industrious for some of the others; had encroached on the natives' domain. But he hadn't really paid much attention to all that.

For a moment he considered making a U-turn where the palm-lined street widened. He could recross the causeway and be home in a few hours. After one seafood meal further inland—he'd promised himself that treat—he could go back. But instead Paul drove on into the small resort.

Carefully Paul parked the large car in front of the tiny Chamber of Commerce building. It was a gaudy storefront concocted of a maze of seashells embedded in cement, their millions of indentations filled with cigarette butts and crumpled foil gum wrappers. Its one cloudy window was filled with colorful brochures.

Paul straightened his tie and brushed his hair in place before he pushed open the door. The light inside was dim, a tint of aquamarine. Nets fuzzy with dust dry-rotted overhead. A wire rack built for a thousand brochures, folders, and maps held a dozen or two dog-eared remnants.

He cleared his throat cautiously and walked to the low counter. On the other side, in a space no larger than a comfortable closet, three people were busy. A thin woman dressed in an out-of-fashion heavy black suit sat talking on the phone, its obsidian receiver matching perfectly her black, looping earrings. Her thin legs were crossed and he noticed the heavy mesh of 1940s stockings, their wide seams almost vulgar. Her shoes, black with stiletto heels, tapped idly against a corner of her desk.

Immediately across the counter a black man with the dry, thin look of a pharaoh's mummy swayed on his broom handle to an internal song.

"Excuse me." Paul heard the unused croak of his voice. He spoke to the third person, directly across from him. She was a gigantic woman; her huge breasts rested on a belly the size of a truck tire.

"Excuse me, miss." Paul felt tired from all of yesterday's madness and this morning's long and dispiriting drive. He wished he were home mowing the lawn or watching Nancy toss a salad. A cool dip in the pool would have done wonders.

The woman rose slowly, her chair moaning. As she crossed the two yards, Paul looked away quickly to the destitute wire rack at his side. As always, he politely avoided witnessing another's misery or pain or misfortune. He was the first to glance elsewhere.

She finally arrived after a struggle with her unwieldy body. Her head barely cleared the counter and she whistled and wheezed. It took another few seconds for her flesh to settle. She spoke between gasps for air.

"Yes sir, can I help you?" Her eyes were miniaturized by her glasses. Paul was caught by them. He'd never seen lenses perform such tricks.

"I'm trying to find a realtor here in town. I'm new. . .just got in. . .we used to come here when I was a child, though. . .years ago." Paul laughed uncomfortably. "Anyway, I'm looking for a beach house to buy. We got his name from a friend but no phone number."

Her tiny eyes tightened as she smiled. "Sure, we can help. Who is it?"

"Louis Bo."

For a second Paul felt everything stop. Only a single tick of the clock. A microsecond gap. The woman on the phone dropped a heel click and the black sweeper broke his sway. The eyes of the huge woman flickered like a cat's.

"Louis Bo's hard to find, you know. He's not even in the phonebook. Very hard to find. Works out of his father-in-law's store in South Crystal." She threw her thick neck in the direction he'd come. "But we've got a dozen other realtors who'd be glad to help." With a sudden flick of her wrist she grabbed a brochure from under the counter and slid it across to Paul. He scanned the list politely.

"Could you give me directions to Louis Bo's store, then?"

"*Louis* Bo," she pronounced the first name as it would be spoken in French. There was obvious disgust in her tone.

Paul glanced at her.

"Listen," she added, leaning across the formica counter as much as her weight would allow her, "we've had years of trouble from all of them, you know. You're from...?"

"San Antonio."

"Yeah, well, you've heard about all the shrimping trouble them people brought in." Her eyes rolled microscopically behind her distorting lenses. "Vietnamese." If she were outside, he felt she would have spat at her feet in contempt.

Paul's stomach tightened. He didn't want any of these problems. Not any of them. "Listen, I'm sorry about all that, really I am. But I don't think it has anything to do with me and buying a house on the beach. Mr. Bo or not." He wiped his forehead with his wilted handkerchief.

The fat on the woman's shoulders heaved and quivered to a stop and Paul realized she must have been shrugging. Deftly she wrote an address on the back of the realtors' list and flipped it across to him. "Vietnamese," she muttered as she turned away.

Outside at the car Paul opened the door but paused. He'd forgotten to ask where the Ramada Inn was. Idly he searched the long strip of downtown for a service station.

"You know what I'd say?"

Paul swung around to see the black sweeper deep in a narrow alley, his head and broom barely discernible.

"What's that?" Paul squinted to see him through the glare of the seacoast sun.

The sweeper glanced over his shoulder and mumbled something.

"What's that?" Paul asked. "I can't hear you."

"I'd say Louis Bo's a fine man. Finer than most here. And something else, too."

"Yes?" Paul shaded his eyes.

"Some houses here just. . .whoosh," and he tossed his free hand skyward.

Paul nodded and sat for a long time in his car with all the air conditioner vents turned toward him.

After checking into the Ramada Inn and eating a mediocre club sandwich in the Inn's restaurant, Paul retraced his drive into South Crystal City. With the help of reticent children's pointing fingers, he found the narrow storefront off the main street facing onto an alleyway that sloped precipitously to the littered oily sand of the bay.

Inside the door he waited for his eyes to adjust, but a minute later he realized they wouldn't. The store was dark except for a weak orange glow from a single lamp near the cash register at the rear.

Paul had to feel his way between the rows of foreign labels — sauces and jars of crystalized spices. He stumbled into a rack packed with pungent seaweed, and thrusting out his hand to right himself, he jammed his forefinger into a solid wall of cans. Quickly he tried to juggle the falling tins but one escaped and rolled across the gritty floor and up under an old box cooler. Paul reshelved the scattered cans and picked his way more slowly.

The concentrated odor of everything on the dark, dusty shelves was almost nauseating.

Finally he reached the counter. It was sandbagged with canvas sacks of rice — thousands of pounds of the stuff buffering the shopkeeper's refuge. "Hello," he said, relieved to have made the journey from the door safely.

"Yes?" A tall old man, dressed in the folds of a blue suit two sizes too large, set a bowl of soup on the counter and stood. The skin of his face hung in loose folds like his suit.

"I've come to see Louis Bo."

The old man's hand abruptly described an arc in the air before him. "Go away. Get out." And, his high voice breaking off, he turned to straighten an immaculate display of rock candy.

Paul started to leave, but he wasn't ready for the troublesome trip back through the groceries. He tried to steel his voice, but it sounded unnaturally high, as reedy and fragile as the old man's.

"I've come to see Louis Bo. I want to see him in person."

"Louis Bo doesn't want to see you, you hear me?" He picked at the display, destroying its symmetry. He didn't look up. His downcast eyes were hidden in the pearly folds of skin. "He's tired of all of this." Again he waved his hand but this time the movement was more subdued, more gentle. "Get out of here. You don't belong here." The old man's voice hissed in the pungent air. He turned his head up, his black eyes glaring. "Go on."

"But listen," Paul wiped his shining face with a sour handkerchief, "I'm not part of 'all of that.' I don't know anything about it. I'm from out of town, you see."

The old man's face trembled and his voice was dry with emotion. "Oh God, then you're the one Louis talked about. You're the newspaper man he said would come and tell the truth about everything. Thank God." The old man started around from behind the counter.

Paul caught the old man's sleeve. "No, no, you don't understand. I'm here to look at a house, that's all. Nothing else."

The shopkeeper's shoulders sagged and he pulled his arm from Paul's grasp.

"All I'm interested in is a summer place for my family. I came here as a child and I've always loved it."

The old man sat heavily on his unpadded stool and poked at his soup with a spoon. For a minute they were quiet. From the street came a rush of language as a crowd of children ran past. Finally, the old man stood again and drew an ancient pen from his suit. He sighed and looked into Paul's eyes. "You don't know how awful it's been." He shook his head and then he shrugged. "Give me your name and phone number. Louis'll phone you later."

After writing his brief message and fumbling his way to the door, Paul looked back toward the dim light. He could barely discern the tall shopkeeper who sat reorganizing the demolished display.

Out in the alley he hardly noticed the bright yellow wrecker whose engine started as he passed it and turned the corner toward his car.

"Hey, you."

Paul didn't hear the man's voice coming from the partially rolled-down tinted window. He noticed the yellow wrecker coasting, keeping abreast of him, but he was thinking of seeing the beach house and returning home as soon as he could—maybe checking out tonight. Then he saw the paradoxical nature of his thoughts. How could he live—even a month out of each year—in a town he was so anxious to leave? He stopped a few feet from his car in amazement. How could he bring his children and Nancy *here*? But he quickly told himself that North Sound would be different—controlled access probably; certainly tight security; walls around each house. But still, there was all of this to avoid. And then he looked up at the yellow wrecker that had stopped, its engine mumbling, almost at his feet.

"Hey, you!"

Quickly Paul stepped back against the low wall that surrounded a dingy house. The palms of his hands brushed the peeling paint.

The low voice, scarcely audible over the noisy motor, came from behind darkly tinted glass. The glare on the windshield was blinding. Paul started to reach for his U.S. Attorney ID to ward off this man, but somehow knew it would just provoke him.

"What do you want?" The rough wood prickled his palms.

"You know Bo, huh? You find him back there?"

"No, he's not there." Paul's words rattled in his dry mouth.

"Why you so interested in Louis Bo?"

"I'm interested in a house he has for sale...on North Sound." For some reason he expected the address to help.

From the cracked window he heard voices, and the static from a CB.

Paul wanted to break and run for his car but he was too old to run away in such heat. Trying to calm himself he noticed details of the wrecker—its elaborate paint work: the rear, hoist and all, a flat black; the rest at least a half-dozen shades of yellow and orange. "Matthew's Wrecker Service" was painted on the door in fancy script.

"It's okay with you if I buy from him?" The firmness of Paul's tone surprised him, but he really was tired and right now all he wanted was the quiet of his motel room. He turned, his palms white from the chalky paint, and walked toward his car.

Slowly the wrecker moved with him.

"You'd be better off with someone else. You know, some-one not Oriental."

"A gook," another voice mumbled and the wrecker filled with harsh, ugly laughter.

"That's my business, isn't it?" Paul spoke softly as he unlocked his car door.

"Maybe so. But you know," the voice came across flat like the monotone of a public-address voice, "you might be better off staying away from Bo and all them goddamned slopes. You hear me?" And with the last word, the window slid up and the wrecker burned rubber, slipped sideways for a second and sped down the quiet street.

Paul laid his head on his arm stretched along the roof of the car. "Jesus Christ," he muttered to the hot, ticking metal.

Once inside his motel room he fastened all the locks and took a long shower, alternating bursts of scalding hot and icy cold water. Then, for a while, he lay on the queen-sized bed with only a towel wrapped around him. He was furious and terrified. And after an hour, he dressed quickly and threw his bag on the barely rumpled bed.

The hell with it, he thought. He'd call Nancy and explain the misery of Crystal City and everything else. She'd get a laugh out of his strange dance with the townspeople.

Now that he'd made his decision, he let the motel room soothe him. As he repacked, he relished its peace and order; the spotless tiled bathroom; the neatly tucked drapes. Every-thing was carefully placed. Even unwrapping a cellophane-sheathed drinking glass brought some comfort.

Crossing over to the phone he stopped and drew the heavy curtains. Beyond the opposite side of the square of rooms, a few dark thunderheads had blossomed inland. Lightning flickered across and through their purple flat bottoms.

As Paul sat on the bed and looked out, the phone purred twice.

"Hello?" he said.

On the other end there was the strange hollow silence one sometimes gets on the phone—the reverberating emptiness of silence in a deep well.

"Mr. Paul Winslow?" The voice was thick and flowed viscous with all the syllables clinging together.

Paul immediately recalled the yellow wrecker and stood to look out the plate glass window and down to the clear blue water of the motel's swimming pool.

"Mr. Winslow, are you there?"

"Yes, yes I am. Who's this?" Paul focused beyond his own reflection in the glass.

"Louis Bo, sir. I hear that you want to look at the North Sound property. It's a good piece of real estate. Very nice. The people who just moved always said. . ."

"I don't believe I'm interested any longer," Paul spoke quickly. "I don't think it's right for us, for me and my family, after all."

"But Mr. Winslow, you've not even seen it yet. How can you know that already? Really, you must give yourself a chance."

Louis Bo talked on, extolling all the house's features, but Paul didn't listen. Instead he watched the pool below. Around it the other guests sat and smoked and drank beer from plastic cups. The middle-aged men's chests sagged; cellulite dimpled the backs of the women's thighs and legs. Children pushed and pulled on the diving board; teetered, screaming, and fell thrashing into the blue of the chlorinated water. It could have been a pool party at his house.

On the highest board a young boy bounced restlessly but never dove. Paul put a hand to the warm glass, the heat of his palm spreading a thin fog outward across the window. For a moment he rested in the scene; in the immaculate, clipped grass and the precisely trimmed hedge.

"So, you see, you owe it to yourself and your family. Don't you think?"

Paul shook his head into the receiver. "I was just about to leave when you called."

"But what can it hurt? And you've come a long ways."

Paul sat on the edge of the bed. He could hear the noises from the pool but they came through the thick glass jumbled and distant.

"Okay. . .I guess so."

For the first time the ingratiating and thick voice laughed—a long, horsey laugh. Then he gave Paul the complicated directions.

After hanging up, Paul set his packed bags near the door and went down to the lobby to check out. But instead he walked past the desk and out into the stifling heat of late afternoon. He sat at an uncomfortable wrought iron table near the pool and drank strong instant tea and sweated through his fresh shirt.

Twice Paul got lost in the intricate maze of sumptuous beach houses. He only relaxed after he found his way and began noticing the sturdy high cedar fences and the carefully kept lawns. Most of the houses were vacant this late in the season, but several showed lights in the dusk.

Cautiously he slowed and stopped before a grand, two-story white house that sat far from the road and right on the beach. As he emerged from the car he delighted in the smack of the waves and the heavy mist blown in on the freshening wind. Overhead he noticed the occasional streak of lightning from the same front of clouds he'd seen earlier from the room.

Paul cupped his hands and bellowed Bo's name over the surf. But there wasn't an answer. And since there weren't any cars close by, Paul tried the massive double gate. The wind tore past him as it swung open. Already he was damp from the heavy mist, his hair plastered flat on his head. The salt trickled onto his lips and into the corners of his mouth.

At the top of the steep stairs Paul rattled the handle of the French doors and tried to peer inside but couldn't make out a thing.

He made a quick circuit of the wraparound balcony, trying windows and doors, but everything was tightly locked and shuttered. On the sea side he sat on the edge of a broken chaise lounge, careful not to tip it. Here the mist was thick. And blown in constantly by the breeze it dripped from the railing in fat drops.

Far off he heard the bass mumble of an engine and the swish of tires on the wet pavement. It sounded like a truck approaching.

"Oh Jesus," he muttered, and walked to the corner near the steps.

He looked down the dark street and through the thickening mist he thought he could discern the silhouette of a truck, the faint glow of its yellow paint and the webbed tackle of its hoist.

"Sonofabitch," he said, loud enough to be heard over the waves below. He tried to wipe away the water and sweat that ran down his face. Under his wet shirt he felt the prickle of his skin.

Edging forward, he reached for the knob again. The loose panes rattled.

Paul's breath stopped for a second. Over the rumble of the surf he believed he heard the slam of a truck door.

Facing the door squarely and pulling his fist back to his chest, he rammed it through the glass as hard as he could. The pain was sharp and immediate but he ignored it and fumbled with the lock inside until the door opened.

Inside he slammed the door and leaned against the glass. The enormous room before him was beautiful. Even in his fear he saw its luxury and comfort—cream carpets, sunken wet bar in a far corner.

But then he felt the sticky flow of blood down his right

arm. Paul brought his hand up close to his face and watched in amazement as it pumped rhythmically from an ugly gash down his wrist and across his palm.

Frantically he searched the house. He ran from room to room hoping to find something to stanch the flow. He trailed the blood everywhere, spoiling the thick carpet and ivory wallpaper.

In the huge, echoing bathroom he twirled the stuck faucets that belched a burst of air and rust.

Then he heard the distinct sound of a door opening. And then the crunch of glass under a shoe.

He stopped with his hands on the taps.

Is this how they felt? he forced himself to ask. This bursting pressure in the ears? This ache in the throat from choking back screams?

Paul glanced up into the dim mirror and could barely recognize his own face distorted and drawn tight across his cheekbones. A swatch of blood colored his forehead and the tip of his nose.

In the mirror was the same fear etched on Shaw's face the instant the grill bit into the back of his head. And standing there he felt that he had broken into some new life and had entered a terrifying and inescapable world.

And there, beyond simple fear, he found rage. He turned from the mirror, ran through the house and lunged headlong into the man standing just inside the door. The force of his lunge carried him and the diminutive man back through the doorway. Screaming, the man sprawled against the rail, and Paul bounded down the stairs. But halfway down he tripped and rolled heavily to the bottom.

For a long time the only sounds were the sea and, above it, their labored breathing.

"Mr. Winslow?" The voice above him was thin with fright. "What are you doing?"

Paul opened his mouth, trying to suck some coolness from

the mist. But his breath came ragged and rasping. And his torn palm began to burn.

"You've ruined my door. Why, you've bashed it in. That's against the law." Mr. Bo stood stiffly and searched his arm for bruises.

Paul turned his head and glanced up and down the street. It was empty except for their two cars.

"What's come over you, Mr. Winslow?" the tiny, meticulously dressed man asked, brushing his rumpled rain-coat. "What's wrong?"

Dazed, Paul shook his head. He started to laugh but couldn't.

"What about my door? What about that?" Louis Bo stood at the head of the stairs and jabbed his finger at the damage.

Paul thought about all the rest of the violence inside, the spotted cream carpet and bloody walls, and nodded his head. Gently, with the tips of his thumb and forefinger, he closed the lips of his wound, but the pain made him wince and he was forced to release the pressure. The blood dripped onto his knee.

Paul wanted to lie back along the hard steps and close his eyes, but he knew that if he did the face in the mirror would return. He turned slowly to look up at the realtor. "Forget about the damage," he said.

"But my beautiful door."

"We'll take it. We'll take the house," Paul mumbled.

"What, Mr. Winslow?" The Vietnamese stepped down the stairs and bent over Paul's upturned face. "I couldn't hear you, sir."

"We want the house."

Bo smiled weakly. "You do?"

Paul nodded and pulled himself up gingerly. After all, he wondered, what else could he possibly say?

MARY sat at the small
desk, the folded letter from Jill in her hands. How much sim-
pler everything would have been, she thought, if she'd written
Jill back days ago and made some excuse. But though she'd
begun a half-dozen times, what could she have written? What
excuse could she have offered that would have canceled Jill's
first visit in over two years?

Mary shook her head and tried to relax her cramped
knees, held tightly together by the child's desk. Then, after
it was too late for a letter to reach Oregon, she'd considered
phoning. But she knew she couldn't do that either. Whatever
the excuse, her voice would have betrayed her. Sitting with
the letter in her hands she recalled that one of her first lies
had been why she'd had the phone disconnected at Papa's—to
save money now that hers was the only income. That had been
easy enough. And since Jill despised calling but loved long,
detailed letters, she'd only had to phone at Christmas and on
Jill's birthday.

But in almost two years of letters, how much had she
invented? How many lies were there?

She carefully extricated herself and stood. She tossed the
letter back on the desk and walked across the room to the
north window. Six steps across. Even though she'd painted
it and built shelves all along one wall, it was still a child-sized
room; her old room. Once it had seemed immense, cavernous. At night there had been dozens of shadowy spots for crea-

tures to lurk in. But now she was just past forty. *Forty-two,* she admitted to herself.

From the window she could see Papa's old house across the wide asphalt road. A car blurred past, scattering two fat chickens and blowing flat for a second the tall Johnson grass that grew right up to the pavement. But Mary didn't blink.

She thought about Scott. She could picture herself over on that far porch — distorted by heat devils undulating already this early in the morning — her face contorted and vicious as he sped off, the gravel slung from the drive rattling against the clapboards.

Sometimes he'd drive into town to drink light beer all night. And other times he'd get up just enough speed to fling the Pinto wagon across the road, through the open gate, scaring her father's few cows, until he lurched to a stop in front of the "new house," as they called it. Then she'd hear the high whine of the saw or the distant chunk of a hammer as he poured his anger into nailheads and mounding sawdust.

Mary pressed her forehead to the glass but from her parents' house she could only see the first row of stunted, twisted pin oaks. She'd lied about that, about the new house. Mary pulled at her face with a hand. Months ago she'd written about the progress she'd been making. How she'd hired a local carpenter who did fine work at a good price.

What else? She needed to sit down and try listing everything. There was the story about the house, about her attempts to get teaching jobs in Austin and Houston. She pictured pages of letters, but she could only remember a few details.

Surely the biggest lie was how she still lived at Papa's house. Mary looked up and across the road. That was the problem now. She gritted her teeth. She'd like to kick herself as hard as she could right in the ass. A letter every week. And now she felt like a child caught by some persistent adult. She couldn't remember when they'd begun. Surely after Scott, but before she'd moved across the road and back home.

"Hey, Sissy Girl!"

Mary turned at her father's voice. "Dad, try knocking once in a while, won't you?"

He gestured with a flick of his wrist and leaned casually against the chest of drawers. He was dressed in his weekend clothes: faded blue coveralls with the company's name—Valley Construction—stitched over the pocket. His pants legs were tucked into the tops of boots white and deeply cracked from neglect.

"When's Jill get here?"

Mary turned away and crossed to sit on the edge of the desk. Her throat felt closed off, her voice was low and hoarse. "Late this evening."

Her father slapped his thigh and shook his head. "Damn...I wish you'd known earlier. Mrs. D and I could have postponed this little vacation. I'd like to see that girl." He grinned and winked at her. "But we'll be back early Sunday, you know. Think she'll still be here?"

"Sure...sure she will. She wouldn't miss you two for anything." Mary looked away.

"Say, I talked to Artie Webber in town...at Sears...and he said they'd be out next Wednesday for sure and start moving it."

Mary looked toward the window and the pin oaks.

"I know it's the best thing. We agreed it was, didn't we, Sissy?"

"Sure."

"And I may as well free up those ten acres. I hate to see it go, too. But it'll never get finished. Hell, he took two years on the shell alone."

"He was meticulous, careful." Mary recalled how he ran

his long fingers down a newly sanded board. But she shook her head slightly. She was over all that.

"Of course he was." Her father was quiet for a moment and then he grinned and reached into his back pocket. "I got the mail."

He walked to her side and edged her over as he rested against the desk.

Mary reached behind them and crumpled Jill's letter.

"Look here, Sissy Girl."

Mary quickly scanned the contract renewal from the local school district.

"And look," her father's stubby finger punched the bottom of the page, "they're upping the ante to keep you. Gives you about a ten percent raise." He dropped the hand with the letter around her shoulder and pulled her up against his chest. She relaxed in his commanding grip, laid her head gently against him.

"Daddy, I wish you wouldn't open my mail. Not even business ones."

"Oh, Sissy, just those. And I really couldn't wait when I saw it was from the school board. I just knew it'd be great news. Hell, wonderful news, isn't it? Another year and more money. You'll save a bundle. No utility bills. Free room and board. And this fall I think we're finally ready to tackle building a deck out back. How about that? Aren't we ready, partner?" He squeezed her hard. She tensed her muscles in response to his. "A nice deck out back for parties and so you and Mrs. D can look out on our 'holdings.'" He released her with a flourish and swept his arms wide. "Our holdings," he repeated.

Mary nodded. "Sure we can. When it gets cooler. With Mrs. D looking on as foreman."

Her father winked at her and walked to the door. "I've got a dozen things to get done before we leave for Galveston; run to the office to file some reports, mow the front yard, pen up the dogs. This was a fine idea of yours. It'll do her good to get out a couple of days. Hell, we haven't been to Galveston in...ten years."

"More like thirty." Mary laughed. Her throat was dry.

"Probably so. Still..." he rapped the doorframe with a knuckle, "I hate to miss old Jilly girl."

"She'll be here. Just get back around noon or so."

He closed the door behind him and Mary sat back down at the desk, the envelope balled in her palm.

She straightened the letter. But she didn't unfold it. In six days she'd memorized it. In one place near the beginning, Jill had said, "We'll miss Scott together." And somewhere farther along she praised Mary for all her ancient college virtues. Only near the close did she mention the quick weekend trip to Dallas to visit a sick aunt and how she'd drive down in a borrowed car. She ended by saying they'd have a marvelous time sitting in her cozy old living room planning her future together.

Her living room. At Papa's house. Mary considered all the elaborate plans that sentence had begun. There'd been the trip to Galveston to arrange. Then the phone call she pretended she got from Jill last night while her parents were at the Elks Club.

"Mary! I've got a surprise for you," Dorothy shouted from the kitchen.

If only she'd come up with some excuse to stop the visit. But as unbeatable at lying as she'd become, she couldn't muster a single line.

Still, it was only one night and morning of Jill. And face-to-face, her voice wouldn't fail her. She'd have to stay at Papa's just tonight.

"Hey, girl, come on in here."

Mary crammed the letter in her jeans. "Coming," she yelled and walked down the hall toward the large kitchen. Everything else she could handle. She'd manage it all somehow.

Dorothy had her back to her daughter, her elbows rough and gray, her hair long and the color of sand.

Dorothy turned and smiled. But Mary looked down to the counter where a neat stack of limes sat in the center of a dish. She looked up at the white-faced clock over the refrigerator. "It's only nine, Mom. That's a bit early, isn't it?" Her voice sounded to her like the dry rattle of litany. Her solo question answered by her mother's flat gaze. Both their parts memorized beyond recognition.

Dorothy shrugged. "He's off to work for a while. What'll it hurt? Besides, it's a special day—vacation day." She turned back to her precise work.

Mary knew the ceremony of the limes. So she sat at the table and flipped through a *Redbook*. In it the rooms were beautiful and tidy and clean. She thought about Papa's house across the road. She hadn't been inside in months now. She knew she should have gone over days ago to begin cleaning. But she hadn't. How could she have explained such a sudden interest? Mary glanced at the clock again. They'd leave at noon. That'd give her a few hours. She looked down at the glossy pictures of cleverly appointed rooms. The knife clicked softly against the cutting board.

Dorothy mounded up the last lime slices. "Your father's supposed to bring back some barbeque from Kruger's for you two girls. Jill's a good ole Texas girl and I know there's no good barbeque in Oregon. Couldn't be, could there?"

Mary closed the magazine and rested her hands on its cover. "I doubt it."

"I want everything perfect for you girls." Dorothy opened the cabinet and took down two glasses. "I still need to vacuum the guest room and dust everywhere else. And change the towels, put out our best."

"You've already packed?"

"Oh no, not yet." Dorothy's voice rose quickly. "But there's time, isn't there?" She glanced at the clock and turned to her daughter. "I'm sure I can get it all done. Can't I, Mary?"

Mary watched her mother's hand on the tile counter. It quivered almost imperceptibly. She felt the letter in her hip pocket and she wanted to stand up and speak, tell her mother the mess she'd gotten into. Ask her help, her complicity in all the lies. Together they'd go over to Papa's and dust and mop. Wash towels and windows.

But that was all impossible. Such confiding always had been. "Don't you worry about it, I'll vacuum and all the rest. You just get packed. That's your only concern."

Dorothy's voice was coming down. "That would be nice of you. Yes, that'd be dear."

She turned back to the glasses and fixed two gin and tonics, carefully following her ritual: gin, ice, twisted lime, tonic. She never stirred it. The limes danced in the bubbles. Dorothy set a drink in front of her daughter and then sat across from her and lit a Salem.

Mary took a long swallow of the bitter drink. She reached down and poked the lime under an ice cube. "You'll have a fine time. It'll be great. The beach. The Galvez is a nice hotel."

Dorothy shrugged and looked around the kitchen. "You'll remember the dogs—you know how your daddy is about them—and that Boston fern, it's on its way out."

Mary smiled and reached to pat Dorothy's hand. "Sure I will. As a matter of fact, I'm considering walking over to Papa's later and giving that old place a good once-over."

Dorothy exhaled the cigarette through her nostrils and shook her head. "Nonsense. It's filthy over there. The electricity's off. . ."

"At the box, not the meter." Mary spoke quickly. Angry, she'd blurted it out. Surprised at herself when everything was going perfectly.

"Hell, it's probably full of bugs. Scorpions. Maybe even *snakes*," she hissed and then took one long swallow emptying the glass.

Dorothy stood and walked over to her drink fixings arranged precisely on the counter. She tilted her head back to finish the last drops of the drink and then poured the ice and spent lime into the dark throat of the garbage disposal.

Mary watched her study the remnants for a moment before she began again: gin, ice, lime, tonic.

"That sorry bastard," she grimaced. "I wouldn't do a god-damned thing to remind myself of him. . .ever. Sorriest bastard in the world."

"Oh, Mom, don't start that again. I'm fine. You know that. It's been over a year now. Well over." Mary looked up at the clock.

Mary took another drink and fished out the lime to pull the bitter fruit from the tough skin.

Dorothy turned and rested her narrow hips against the brown tile of the counter. She looked at her daughter and suddenly grinned. "Of course you're fine. And here you are. The 'junior partner,' as your father says. And my old girlfriend." She nodded and swirled the drink.

Mary looked down at her empty glass. "But you do know it's too early for your 'breakfast.' You promised never before eleven."

Still grinning, Dorothy crossed over to stand behind Mary, her free hand rearranging her daughter's hair.

Mary sat up straight and stiff as she always had when her mother fixed her hair or approached her from behind to zip a dress or adjust a blouse.

"You never told in high school." Dorothy ran a thumb along Mary's jaw. "We've always kept secrets, you and me. That's why we're girlfriends. You and me and Jill."

The ice in the glass at Mary's ear clinked and the tonic

fizzed. She nodded and reached up to pat her mother's arm. Once, she recalled, after a full week of rain, Scott had found a tangled wad of scorpions under the stereo. She'd watched from the window as he dumped them in the charcoal grill and doused them with gasoline. That night and for several in a row, she'd been afraid to stretch her feet out to the end of the bed and she'd nestled up against his back.

They didn't leave until one. Mary practically packed them in the car and shut the doors. Dorothy bunched a pillow behind her head and closed her eyes. Her father jerked a thumb up and fishtailed on the gravel driveway, squealed out onto the road.

Hurriedly Mary gathered a sack full of food: the barbeque, chips, cans of Coke. In another paper bag she piled cleaners, a bar of soap, fresh towels and sheets.

Loaded, she crossed the asphalt road but stopped on the yellow center stripe. Her parents had disappeared to the south. Looking northwards, she could see empty road for a couple of miles. She looked back at her parents' house and wished she could spend the afternoon and night reading some of the newer magazines. Or sketching some ideas for the deck.

Reluctantly she turned towards Papa's to flip on the electricity at the side of the house.

When she opened the door at the old house, a wave of stale air met her. She inhaled the entombed air, a concoction of disuse and dryness. "Oh, shit," she exclaimed and, bending slightly, she set the groceries on the desk inside the door. Then she walked to the center of the small living room.

The oval rug under her feet cast up dust as fine as flour. The windows over the bookcases were dim with grime and streaked by rain. And in the corners were long, hanging tendrils of cobwebs. Her quick survey took the air from her like a jab to the abdomen. She sat on the coffee table. Drops of perspiration fell on the table's glass top and she traced circles through the thick fuzzy layer of dust.

She looked over at the groceries and towels and shook her head slightly. If the living room was all this bad, she wondered, how awful's the bathroom? And she'd have to wash all the damned dishes. Turn on the refrigerator. She slammed a fist down on the tabletop and after a few seconds she did it again more purposefully and forcefully. How the hell could she even begin? Much less make the damned dirty place look like she'd never left it months ago?

She raised her head and shifted on the table to look through the far doorway to the front bedroom. She could see the foot of the bed. And the scarred chest of drawers. Something skittered across the floor and Mary jerked up off the table and stepped to the center of the rug. She thought of her mother's mention of snakes. Christ only knew what lived in here now. Maybe spiders. She glanced around, trying quickly to probe the shadows under the couch and bookcases. Squatting, she peered under the stereo. But there were no scorpions. She didn't see a thing.

Mary stood and stepped gingerly to the front windows and, wetting her fingertips, wiped a circle in the yellow grime. Her parents' house stood cool and white back under the oaks. She noticed that her father had left the porch light burning.

But her letters said she lived here, not over there. And that she lived here alone and happy. And after all, it was only for this day and night and a bit of tomorrow morning.

Turning to face the room she shuddered. Jill could expect some dusty books, smudged glasses, a cobweb here and there. She'd never been that neat. She took a deep breath of the hot heavy air and rushed through the house pulling up all the windows not painted shut. Then she vacuumed, thrusting the rattling wand far up under chairs and into closets, hoping to chase out anything hiding in the dark.

Some things she left alone. The glasses only needed a quick swipe with a damp cloth. The refrigerator exhaled a deep dirty smell like spoiled beer, but she turned it on maximum cold and hoped the chill would somehow take the edge off the fetid odor.

Once into the work, into the methodical plan she'd quickly laid out, she thought about nothing else. Only how to get the small house looking as if she'd never moved across the street; as if she'd been here every night the last ten months.

She left the streaked bathroom mirror alone. She dusted the bedroom vanity table meticulously and laid out some old combs and nearly empty bottles of perfume. She was afraid to light the water heater though she finally managed, thinking of Jill's surprise about a cold shower. And she exchanged the puckered gray roll of toilet paper for a fresh one.

This is for you, Jill, she kept thinking as she scrubbed rapidly or swept the cobwebs from the corners, raising a cloud of greasy dust. This is for you, she thought, until it became a refrain as automatic and constant as chewing gum on a long drive—the mind, like the jaw's muscles, working furiously at nothing. She was sure she was completely over Scott; now the house, though still full of her belongings, didn't stir a single memory. Only the cleaning and thoughts of Jill's arrival occupied her mind. It was like cleaning some stranger's house.

This is for you, Jill. She bunched the drapes back and tied them with their elastic cords in order to hide their dirty stained bottoms that had been soaked through a cracked windowpane. *This is for you.*

At four o'clock she stopped and carefully inspected each room. It was okay, she nodded, it would have to do. Jill had written she'd be there by five or so. And even though she was usually late for everything, Mary couldn't chance it.

She closed the windows and turned the two air conditioners on super-cold. The windowpanes rattled and the first burst of air was a barrage of lint and dried insect bodies.

Mary unpacked the groceries, put the Cokes in the freezer, and took the sheets and towels to the bathroom linen closet. Then, collecting a decent change of clothes from the ones she'd left here, she stripped off her sweaty shirt and filthy jeans and stepped under the shower.

She took a long drink of cold water from the rush of the showerhead but she couldn't quench her thirst, wet her dry mouth. The pages of the letters ran through her head. Besides living here, what else had she said? She'd written about looking for jobs. No, she'd said she'd applied for some this spring and expected to hear soon. Mary nodded. And there had been something about the new house. Not only that she was having it finished. Some damned thing about landscaping the whole yard around it. But was that done or going to be next summer? Thank God it was still there. Its move she could handle later.

Turning, she let the pounding spray prickle her shoulders. Whose business was it where she lived anyway? Here or over there. Or if she'd decided to sell the new house and have it moved. It doesn't matter. Of course it doesn't. She stretched her head back and let the water drench her hair. I'm old enough to do what I want.

Mary turned and finished rinsing herself. Stepping from the shower she heard a loud knock at the door. Her wet body tensed and she felt flushed all over despite the cold shower.

She quickly scrubbed dry and wrapped a towel around her soaking hair. She cursed as her wet skin resisted the blue jeans.

The knock was louder. Mary misbuttoned the blouse and trotted to the door. Through the gauze curtain she made out Jill's bulky silhouette. Tightening her cheeks into a smile, Mary opened the door.

Jill's green eyes took Mary in from face to feet to face again and then the corners of her large mouth folded into a smile that puckered her crow's-feet. "You old thing," she murmured and reached out to draw Mary to her across the threshold, "how the hell are you?"

Mary worried that Jill might feel her thumping heart through her damp blouse. She dropped her arms around Jill's neck and patted her back. "I'm fine, just fine. And you're early for once." And then she hugged Jill like a man. "Oh, Jilly, it's so good to have you here again." Mary was surprised at her own sudden emotion.

"Hey," Jill released her and stepped back a foot to look over Mary's shoulder and into the room. Mary felt her stomach knot and clenched her fists involuntarily. She was afraid to turn and follow Jill's gaze.

"Hey, this is great. You've done something in here since my last visit. What is it?" Jill took Mary's arm and walked into the room slightly ahead of her. "What's new?" Jill led her around the small room stroking her forearm comfortingly. She stopped before the freshly waxed secretary. "This is, isn't it?"

"I think so," Mary stuttered. "Scott and I bought it right before the separation."

Jill nodded and led Mary to the dusty old couch and pulled her down at her side. "I'm sorry. I guess we do need to mention it; we can't help it."

Mary disengaged her arm and inched away to turn and face her old friend. Jill's forehead was wrinkled, her voice low and soothing.

"Come on, I'm fine about that. I really am. Hey, want a Coke?" Mary stood and watched a cloud of dust rise from the couch. Jill didn't seem to notice.

"Sure. . . listen, I'll go get my stuff, okay? You fix the Cokes and I'll bring in my *toilette*." She laughed at her theatrical French accent.

"You don't need any help?" Mary smiled and reached down to take a hand and help her up. They stood together.

"Nope, not a bit. The older I get, the less stuff I pack.

Mind you, the more I need"—she brought a finger up to the deep wrinkles on her forehead—"but the less I could give a shit."

"That's a girl." Mary reached and touched the creased forehead. "But you are as beautiful as you were twenty years ago. I'm glad you're here."

Jill's eyes ranged Mary's face. "And you're no better at lying than you were. And I'm glad I'm here too." Jill arrested Mary's hand and held it.

Mary almost spoke.

"Go get the drinks, girl. We have a lot of bullshit to catch up on. Time for cigarettes and bullshit, huh?"

Mary nodded emphatically and walked to the kitchen. She listened to Jill return to her car as she opened the freezer. The rubber gasket along the door's edge was black with mildew and the refrigerator still smelled terrible. Mary took out the Cokes and lifted out an ice tray. But the only ice was the thin skim along the rim of the cups.

"Hey, where do I drop this stuff? Which room?"

Mary brought down two fairly clean glasses and began gently breaking the slivers of ice. "It doesn't matter. Wherever."

"Sure it does. I don't want to run you out of yours. It's still the big back room, huh?"

"Sure. Yeah, you take the front one. Yell if you need anything." She hoped the Cokes were cold enough to leave some ice unmelted.

Mary heard Jill bumping her luggage against furniture. She listened now, her hand slippery on the sweating red can. She heard Jill open the closet door to put up her hanging clothes. Mary, thinking of the scurrying shape, waited for a shriek. But there was only the faint jingle of clothes hangers. She finished pouring the drinks and went back in.

"Is it cool enough for you? I've had the air conditioners off during the morning. You wouldn't believe last month's bill. Christ almighty. Oregon's surely cheaper on electricity."

Jill took a long drink of her Coke as they sat on the couch, their legs tucked underneath them, facing one another. Mary looked away toward the front windows. She'd only managed to smear the grime around. The corners of each pane were still blurry.

"When do we get to see Mrs. D and your dad?"

Mary looked down into the drink, at the bubbles ascending in long chains of beads. "They were so upset." She looked up, focusing on Jill's lips. "But Daddy had a meeting—some business about new tax codes or something like that—and he took Mrs. D with him. They won't be back until Sunday night. Mrs. D was really counting on seeing you." Mary shrugged.

"That's too bad." Jill finished her drink and set it on the coffee table. "But how're they doing?"

"Oh, just great. He's as busy as ever with his cows and everything. A dozen different projects going at once. She's just fine."

"Hey, I saw the house." Jill half stood to look through the windows. "Yep, you *can* see it from here. It looks good. Why don't we walk over later and take a look? You've said so much about what you've managed to get finished since last winter. Renting it seems a really fine idea. Hey, any word yet on jobs in Austin?"

Mary felt smothered by all the talk. She hadn't recovered from the frantic cleaning. The shower had ended too suddenly and had enervated rather than fortified her. And now things were accumulating just as she had feared they would. She'd taken care of her parents. Now she'd have to maneuver around the house. The shell of it unpainted and cracking. The inside still unfloored, weeds arching over the floor joists. And she didn't remember saying anything about renting it out.

She took a sip of the sweet liquid. "No word yet about a job. You know Austin ISD must get a million applications every spring." Leave me alone, she wanted to say. "Maybe we can go over to the house after it cools off some."

"Speaking of cooling off, Aunt Babe's car has no AC. Not even the vent fan works. So, could I get a quick shower and then we'll really let loose? How about that?"

"Of course." Mary set her Coke down and stood. "Come on and I'll remind you where the towels are."

In the bathroom Jill stripped off her clothes and bent to adjust the water. Mary gathered her stuff up and went in to spread it on the bed.

"Say, I've been having some trouble with the hot water heater. There may not be much hot water."

Jill spoke over the hiss of the shower. "That's fine. I'd love an icy bath. It'll be just the thing."

Mary sat heavily on the bed and listened to Jill hum under the water. Her own hair was still damp and she unwrapped it and reached for an old brush she'd laid out on the bureau. But she didn't have the energy to drag it through the thicket of tangles.

"You don't know this, it just happened." Jill turned the water off. "But I have a new man in my life. Happened a week ago. He's the new Speech Department head. I can't tell you what he's like. Nothing at all like Jim, thank God."

Mary sat up straight on the bed. "Oh? But you were really in love with Jim, weren't you? Despite all his complicated games, wasn't he the most important one in years?"

Mary sucked her bottom lip and ran her fingers through the prickling bristles of the brush. She recognized a path through the dangerous mesh of lies. She should have recalled Jill's penchant for detailing her own elaborate life.

"Sure, he was something all right. But this man. . .wait'll you hear about this one." Jill laughed as she dried off with one of the freshly laundered towels.

Mary began brushing her hair, counting the strokes. "Tell me everything. Every detail. Don't leave a thing out."

"But first," and Jill stuck her head around the doorframe, "let me say how proud I am of you. You made it through. Goodbye Scott. Hello Mary's new life. And you look great." She jabbed a finger emphatically at Mary. "I knew you'd be fine."

Mary nodded and continued brushing. "But let's talk about this fellow of yours."

And they did talk about him. And later, over greasy but "marvelous" barbeque, as Jill kept saying between huge bites, they backtracked through their lives. So, in the living room again, at ten, with the local news playing silently behind them—Jill wanted to see what tomorrow's weather would be like for her long drive back to Dallas—Mary talked about Scott. Then in the kitchen at midnight, over cups of dark thick coffee, they remembered their college days together. They recalled when they'd first met Scott—actually Jill had met him in an intro government class first and he'd tagged along one hot September afternoon for a free beer at their duplex. And Mary'd twisted off the sweaty cap for him as he'd pushed back suavely in the rickety wooden chair and wound up on the floor in a flood of beer foam.

The two laughed over that. Recalled the other men who'd come and gone in those days. Remembered the campus demonstrations Mary'd slept through while Jill carried a placard of some gruesome photograph of napalmed bodies and chanted against Johnson and McNamara.

They always moved backwards, though the conversation often leapt forward a year or five to fill in the latest news about divorces, a suicide, a marriage. And, as the unwinding of their history took Mary constantly away, farther and farther, from

Papa's house, her parents', the dark unpainted shell a half-mile away to the east, she soon relaxed. There in that already lived past she was free of the entanglements and complications. She didn't fear tripping herself up.

Finally, at two, they both yawned simultaneously and deeply and then looked at one another and broke out in laughter. By now they were sprawled on the wide bed in the front bedroom.

"Oh Lordy, my aching back. We'd better get some sleep. I'll have to leave by eight or nine at the latest." Jill stood and stretched languidly.

Mary agreed and stood too. "I'll just wash up the glasses."

"I'll help."

Mary shook her head and reached down to turn back the covers. "You get in here and write the new man the postcard you've been threatening all night. Go ahead and tell him all you're worried about."

"And excited about?"

"That too." Mary deftly plumped the terribly flat pillows. "I'll drop back by and give you a big hug."

She walked through the small house turning off lights, adjusting the thermostat on the air conditioner, collecting the pile of saucers and glasses. In the kitchen she ran the sink half-full of sudsy hot water and looked at her reflection in the long narrow window over the counter. Dropping her hunched shoulders and relaxing the aching muscles of her face, she realized how knotted-up she'd been. Mary tossed her head in relief and carelessly swished water over the dishes. Soon she began humming a Bob Dylan song—the words she couldn't recall—but something from her college days inspired by their talk.

"Mary?"

She turned around. "What? What's wrong?"

Jill's face was puzzled, her forehead wrinkled. She took a step into the kitchen but stopped. "I don't know. . . but. . . I forgot the date—for the postcard—and went to the calendar in the bathroom. Then I found one in the hall...in the secretary."

Mary turned back to the dishes, her fingers worked themselves through the loose net of the dishrag. Looking up she saw Jill distorted in the steamy window. The white blur of the calendars showed in a lower pane. The adults had found her out. She opened her mouth to answer and saw herself in the window, actually watched herself unable to think.

"Mary?" Jill's voice was now small and very quiet. "Mary, all the calendars are last year's...March...the month Scott moved out. I..."

Mary bowed her head and waited to cry, expected some tears to form. But instead the word *calendar* caught in her mind and she bent over and began to laugh.

"Goddamned calendar. Oh shit, Jill, a stupid simple damned calendar." And she turned toward Jill's frightened face. Now the tears did come but she thought they were because of her laughter.

Jill's face softened and she walked over and led Mary to the table. She sat down gently and hooked a chair with her foot and pulled it to her. She sat at Mary's elbow and caressed her hands.

Mary shook her head and breathed deeply. She felt relieved. "I don't know exactly how to begin all this. But all my letters..."

Jill brushed Mary's wet cheek with her lips. "Oh, Mary, I knew the divorce hit hard. I've felt it all along. That you were in pain but brave about it all. I sensed something in your letters full of plans—good ones—but still, you seemed so distant, distracted. And I couldn't help notice," and she swept her hand around the kitchen, "the neglect. But I understand now. How the whole business put you in a state." Jill laughed encouragingly. "Hell, I'm a terrible housekeeper and I haven't been through a bit of the shit you have. That damned Scott."

As Jill talked on, Mary's first feelings of relief were shoved aside by a second route of escape. Clearly and plainly it lay before her blazed and charted by Jill's words. She could take it easily enough. Yes, Jill, it has really been hard. Of course Jill, I have been upset. Too much so to notice outdated calendars or to care about dusty corners, mildewed gaskets.

Mary closed her eyes and relaxed in Jill's embrace. Tomorrow she'd be back across the highway. Her father full of plans for her future. Her mother celebrating the ceremony of the limes with her as if she were still in high school and had never gone away. For a moment, in her mind, she saw all three of the houses as if she were somewhere a mile off and standing alone on a hillside. There was this house, Papa's house, that she had abandoned one afternoon late because she simply didn't belong here anymore. And there was the new house that never would be finished and in a few days would be moved away.

She wanted to tell the truth about the calendars and all the houses and everything else. But from the hill she saw the third house with its porch light burning in the dark.

She opened her eyes and blinked. Jill's arms tightened around her shoulder. Then, she stood and leaned with her knuckles on the table.

"What is it?" Jill stood alongside her.

Mary crossed over to the sink and turned on the tap to rinse the dishes. "I'm okay now. Really I am." She heard Jill sit noisily at the table behind her.

"Let's talk some more, okay?"

Mary dried the glasses. Out of the corner of her eye she noticed the calendars that Jill had laid on the edge of the counter. Wiping her hands on her shirttail, she reached over for them and turned to face her best friend.

"I guess the divorce was awfully upsetting. And living alone hasn't always been easy."

Jill nodded and then beamed at her. "But you *will* recover fully. A new job in Austin'll help. Or. . . hey!" Jill thumped the table decisively. "You can come out to Oregon for a while. Next month'll be great! We can take off for the coast or the mountains. Or both. There's a fine little hotel I know of in Coos Bay." She nodded in satisfaction. "That's just the ticket. It really is."

Mary turned away from Jill and, laying the calendars on the flour canister, she opened the cabinet and began putting up the dishes. "Sounds really fine. I think I'd like that. But I just know they're going to offer me something in Austin any day now. And I'll have to be here for the interview. I couldn't afford to miss it."

Mary looked over her shoulder and smiled. "But after that, maybe so. I'll write as soon as possible with all the latest news from the Lone Star State."

Leaving the Italian Alps

I only sort of lived at home in '72. I kept my clothes there, let Mother do the wash, came in sometimes coinciding with the old man's departures. He'd be climbing into the Kenworth on his way to pick up a load of lumber and I'd crunch to a stop almost on his bowed legs.

I'd be drunk or on the shitty side of sobriety and he'd shout as I stumbled out of the car and latched onto a fender for support. He'd sarcastically tell me I had to be at work in an hour; remind me how he'd managed to finagle me the job. Finally he'd warn me not to wake my mother who stayed up late every night worrying and went to bed after deep, earnest prayers asking for the redemption of her heathen son and his godless friends.

Then he'd pull out and I'd walk around to the trunk, open it, take the fifth of Cutty Sark out of its cradle of old work clothes in the wheel of the spare tire, uncork it—I'd searched hard, two counties away, for Cutty bottles with corks like they had in *Carnal Knowledge*—and throw back a manly slug that boiled in my throat, fought its way to my stomach, and blossomed there in an orange flower of indigestion at five in the morning. "Bastards," I'd say. "Lousy bastards." Both of them. I'd moved back after my abortion of a semester at college—though I wouldn't dare tell anyone, I was lonely and in love with a girl who'd gone away to the University of Illinois—and exposed myself to Mother's vehement religious blasts and the old man's pride at having rescued his smart-assed but failed student-son. Though it had slacked off between us some after six months, and she seemed to have given up on my soul and I'd learned to tolerate the fiberboard plant the way you live with back pain. And the fucking money was certainly okay.

I was white, nineteen, and it was summer. It was '72 and I'd been born right and missed Vietnam. And after dark in an East Texas sawmill town of twenty thousand a young man could give way to almost all his urges. Could I have remained my own creation?

Maybe I'd fuck all night—though the pickings twenty miles up the road in Ore City weren't all that great. More likely I'd smoke two packs of Chesterfields and drive 150 miles to Patroon or on into Louisiana with Don Campbell to buy more Scotch in corked bottles.

The Camaro'd do 140 easy with its bored 327, Borg-Warner four-speed, and 3/4 race cam. In high school I'd had a decrepit piss-yellow Renault. But this fucker could go. And I went. We all did, cramming into the car, Don riding shotgun. The Scotch opened and sloshed into Dallas Cowboys mugs, somebody in the back smoking dope. No one died; we never even got tickets.

We'd probably end up at Kate's apartment some time after midnight. I had a key. Don did too. A few dozen of us did. Kate lived with Lisa and both were students at Clayburg Community College. And that year, for some reason, their place was where the parties started like spontaneous combustion.

So we'd drift in at all hours. The parties, like the driving, were held pedal to the floor. The guys who showed up had gone straight into the lumber mills or the foundries. They'd been fucking and drinking hard for years now. I'd never been wild in high school—that's why Don and I hadn't run with the same crowd; why I'd received a scholarship to college. I'd never really been very drunk save a couple of times like after graduation and over some of the big football weekends at college. But in '71 I began practicing with a vengeance and in a few months I had quite a reputation.

Sometimes Don and I showed up at Kate's and no one was there in the large old garage apartment at the very end of the street in North Ore City near the foundries. Then we'd just sit on the balcony and continue our drinking and look out over the wire-topped fences and rows of crane-like pumping units to the constant blur of huge window fans that ran all year and whose blades reflected the golden glow of the furnaces. Don worked in their marine bearings division.

But we seldom sat quietly for long. The nights were vital. Full of speed and noise and frantic activity. Who'd drive? Who'd come along? And the crowd at Kate's would change imperceptibly or quite suddenly. That fall Don drove up to Alaska looking for work but a month later he returned flat broke, with a Folger's can full of glacial pebbles and enough stories to last for months. Right after that Allen Lott came back from the war with a buddy, Sonny Parker. And after Sonny showed up, things changed.

For him, Vietnam was "good fucking dope" and "a total shit, a total fucking shitass sort of place." I'd nod. Don would suck in his cheeks. We'd be sitting on the balcony over the driveway and sometimes the cops'd cruise by and shine their spots our way. Once Sonny Parker stood up and slowly bowed like some mechanical toy. We cheered nervously but his face didn't register a thing. Later that night I'd held some girl's head over the john while she puked the twentieth time, the smoke and music loud as ever, a dozen people talking in the small living room, the narrow hall just outside the bathroom crowded with lawn furniture one of the guys had lifted from the country club. And Sonny Parker came in, stepped over us and pissed in the bathtub. I looked up to see him adjusting his shirt, the skin on his back and sides completely covered with tattoos—

ships, airplanes, women, their breasts huge and distended.

As winter came on, I crossed Sonny Parker's path more and more. I'd come into Kate's with Don in tow, our arms loaded with cheese from Safeway and sausage and half-gallons of Chianti. Or else barbeque from Milton's, the brown paper sacks shiny and dark with grease.

We'd speak to the others. People'd nod across the room. Someone would turn the stereo up. CCR's "Proud Mary." Or Don McLean's "American Pie." Sonny Parker would emerge from one of the bedrooms with Lisa. My expert eye on her face and then his. Often we locked gazes for a while in some childish game. I had no idea why. The dope smoke a pure blue in the candlelight or yellow along the seams around the bathroom door.

It was nothing ever said. I'd speak later in the kitchen scooping ice into an old cup I always left in the drain rack. And he'd mumble back, his face simply acknowledging my voice, my presence.

When he didn't show up I thought I sensed some lessening of the pressure in the room as if stagnant air had been refreshed by an opened window. People talked louder, acted more themselves—got drunker, rowdier. I talked Don into standing in the driveway below and, leaning far out over the balcony railing, a couple of girls holding my ankles and knees, I swung an empty champagne bottle against his electric-blue motorcycle helmet. The bottle didn't break—the helmet either, which was the purpose of our drunken experiment. But Don was catapulted backwards into the bright green holly. We all tumbled down the steps to haul him out and ended up wading deep into the sharp leaves to drag him onto the driveway.

Sonny's presence dampened such exploits. He was only a bit older than Allen Lott, who was almost Kate's age. But he carried more substance, more weight. And somehow something murky and less resilient than all the rest of us. His fragility got on our nerves.

There were rumors. When he didn't show, someone would turn up the music. Lisa would dance with Don. Someone would say something about what they'd just heard. How Sonny had a kid in Odessa he'd never seen, or how he'd been fired from the Nueces Foundry for stealing tools and selling them. The guy claimed he'd bought a set of sockets from Sonny for next to nothing. Once Allen told Don how easy they'd had it in Vietnam. They spent the whole tour at Tan Son Nhut Airfield in Graves Registration stamping and filing papers, strapping the caskets on pallets, directing the forklift operators. Only at the very end had the monotony been broken by rocket attacks. Though later, to me, Allen wondered if maybe it hadn't somehow helped fuck Sonny up—their exhausting nights under the halogen lamps, planes in and out, more care spent accounting for the boxes than had been spent on the grunts in them. But Allen shrugged it away. Sonny had had a miserably poor childhood in South Texas, around Harlingen. Now he simply moved from woman to woman; lived here and there with anyone who'd put up with his bullshit moods. He prided himself on having only a single brown bag full of possessions.

Allen was okay; someone who'd made it back intact. But for us Sonny was some sort of weird by-product of Vietnam. After all, TV was populated with vets who came back with strings of ears, the jitters, and vivid dreams of firefights that led inevitably to arson, hostage-taking, murder. Sometimes Ironside rescued them from themselves. We accepted such broad brushstrokes. When he wasn't around we called him G.I. Joe, or just Joe.

We weren't about to let such stuff get us down. We gave all such things a healthy shove. The dope abetted. And the Cutty; the often entangled relationships.

But one night at Kate's I stepped over someone in dirty coveralls and spoke to Sonny, laid my hand on his arm. The girl he had cornered took the opportunity to slide away. Her eyes glazed, she held onto a brass floor lamp for support.

"Why don't you let her go on home? She's really wasted."

Sonny turned his face from the light, the side toward me in dark eclipse.

"Why don't you just fuck off? Why don't you try that, you little prick?"

But for some reason I edged around him and took her hand off the lamp. I must have been someone else for a moment: it was the action of a book's hero—something from *The Sun Also Rises*—something read or more likely seen. People who say movies don't affect us are pretty goddamned stupid. Jack Nicholson took the stoned girl's arm, led her past "the heavy," the cruel vet with his ear necklace, and navigated her down the steps and into her mother's clunky station wagon.

I bounded back up the steps and opened the door to the noise. Walking right up to him (he stood by the wobbly, soaked drinks table), Nicholson looked him straight in the eye. My vague dislike turned to hatred and backed me up. "If you want to take this outside, we can." The Duke spoke. I thought I saw Allen Lott's head turn toward me admiringly. I definitely watched as Sonny's hand fell and grabbed a Mateus bottle.

All the rest jumbled together. People yelling. Kate crying close to my ear. Lisa driving me to the emergency room, the scalp lacerations soaking my jeans with blood down to my pockets, coloring her upholstery. Don babbling with the orderlies and nurses, handing them my wallet and insurance card.

In truest form I was too numb with booze to feel a thing. And again in true form, I only threw up into the stainless steel kidney pan after my mother arrived. The old man was out of town.

"Just look at you!" she said on the way to x-ray. "If you could see what I'm having to see."

Later Don came back from the extinguished party to sit across the bed from Mother in the only other metal chair in my room.

He had on the top hat he always wore to parties, and after a rambling incoherent account of my beating, his head dipped and the hat rolled up under the bed.

"You'd better go home," Mother leaned over me to direct her hiss at Don's unfocused grin.

"Where'd my hat go?" he asked us, but Mother'd already bent to kick it out from under the bed and all the way to the door.

Later she knelt by the bed and grabbed my arm. Turning her moon-face upwards and into the fluorescent light like Bernadette at Lourdes, she invoked the wrath of God, targeted my heathen friends—Don in particular—named their supposed sins as if she were spotting for God's artillery, phoning in coordinates from high ground.

I fortunately had the good timing of needing the kidney bowl for another bout of vomiting. Mother held my head, sighed repeatedly at the spectacle, and finally left, threatening to bring the old man next time.

I had a slightly detached retina; they taped a Fox patch over my left eye (one of those uncomfortable but romantic metal jobs with holes in it) though even with it closed, I still saw colorful displays of ball bearings rotating frantically.

Mother sent the Baptist preacher by—I tried to insult his pretentious, silly views of good and evil, but his smugness and ignorance had overwhelmed any remaining intelligence years ago. And the old man did drop by, alone, baseball cap in hand, to shake his head and grin. "Two shiners, huh? He got you good." His tone was too happy to miss.

But mostly I lay in bed in misery. Not from pain though. My head never did hurt and the scalp wounds didn't require sutures. My neck ached some. But lying perfectly still and staring out the window my first morning, I considered my ruined reputation. More Wally Cox, Barney Fife than Nicholson. I'd walloped kids in junior high, but lately it'd been bravado and boast. I'd been freewheeling and devil-may-care. Looking in the mirror at the silver patch taped across my eye, the tape running over the bridge of my nose and to my temple, I felt my stock plummeting. I figured few of them had seen such a beating before and word'd get around until everyone knew.

I shaved in the afternoon, the black tile cool on my feet. And I didn't look at my one good eye but instead glided the razor over the bruises, wiped the final fleck of blood off the bridge of my nose. It would be difficult to face all of them again. I doubted I had the nerve or energy.

I hated Sonny Parker. The G.I. Joe'd gone berserk. He'd batted me around like some dumb punching bag in front of everyone. He'd given Mother fresh ammunition in the battle for my soul just when we'd achieved an uneasy armistice. The old man could come out of retirement and live for months with his grin and shake of a head. God knew what everyone else thought.

So I began to plot terrible retribution. I imagined maiming Sonny; hiding in the dark of a hedge and leaping out at him, tire iron in hand. I'd hurt him terribly, or choose my moment carefully and humiliate him in front of everyone at Kate's.

When he opened the wide oak door after my dinner and tapped on its inside lightly, my hatred surged, left the scale because I recognized my fear of him. I realized my body'd tensed, my toes were straight out under the tight hospital sheets. Imperceptibly I'd edged nearer the pale blue wall. He's here to finish me off, I thought, and actually considered it possible he had one last wine bottle in his other, obscured hand.

"Hey man, you okay?" His young-old face was puzzled. We both were. My left hand had wadded up the folds of the sheet. I put the other palm up flat as if to say "How" like Indians do in westerns. Whatever I meant by it, he stayed just inside the door, still holding its heavy weight open.

"You know, I'm awfully sorry." He couldn't look directly at me. Instead he looked down at his hand on the doorknob and then, if he looked up at all, he only brought his eyes up, kept them hidden under his eyebrows. It was something vague, almost animal-like. A defense used by children or primates. I looked away to the mirror over the washbasin. The Gillette reminded me of my shave and hatred.

"I just wanted to let you know I'll pay for all this. Anything you need . . . Hey . . ." But his words only sounded as if they should propel him into the room, to the metal chair near my nightstand. "You won't press charges, will you? Have you called the cops?" He was almost whining.

So that was it, I thought. And all the hatred I'd cultivated so earnestly all day refined itself into disgust. I felt grand and in a bit of pain and in control. So I didn't speak. Instead I simply turned over. But I didn't shut my eyes as I wanted to. The fear was still there. He'd hit me once; my back and ass felt a mile wide. I realized my skimpy gown was probably open.

I'm no more a coward than the rest. I would like to have stood, walked over and struck him hard enough to smash teeth and bones. But I already knew his ability. I considered turning away the nobler act; a disdain for him that would eventually soak into his G.I. Joe mind somehow. It was safer, I figured, than any foolish alternative. I didn't speak because I was sure my voice would quiver and break.

For a long time I looked at the wall, my breathing under a conscious and iron control. My backside defeating him, I waited for a change in the air pressure that would signal the door closed. Something had to happen. If I turned over and he was still there, we'd have to begin again and this seemed out of the question.

"Damn but that's a beautiful sight," Don said and slapped my ass a stinging blow.

"Goddammit, man!" I yelled and sat up. Over his shoulder I saw the grinning faces of a half-dozen friends. Behind them all was the sour gaze of the floor RN.

And for the next few days, the RN acted the librarian, her stubby finger constantly to her lips shushing us. And we partied as quietly as possible. Because they weren't any of them ashamed of me. In truth my popularity soared. Even Allen Lott had come by to condemn Sonny, to shake his burr head, his fatigue cap twirling in his hands. Lisa came by with flowers and avoided mentioning his name. Don brought Kate with him and she told me Sonny and Lisa were still together, but barely. Kate had moved out to another girl's mobile home until things got better.

Mother quit coming the day she opened the door and saw Don, top hat on, dealing a round of seven-card stud on my clean but patched sheet. She had some church tracts in her hand and she tossed them at us as she left. They whirled in a flurry in the strong draft from the air conditioner.

Even some guys from work stopped by though I'd never hung out with them. They talked about my fight and asked about the condition of the other fighter. I only grinned. That's what everyone was calling it now—a fight.

I returned to my glory. We played cards, smuggled beer in, tossed the empty cans up under the bed. I even made serious passes at the dietician who was in her thirties and came around to ask me if I could stand any more fried shrimp or if I preferred the lime jello with canned pears. I'd read *A Farewell to Arms*, and the day before I left I reached out and took her hand and she sat at the head of the bed. We looked out the window and I imagined the snow-capped Italian Alps beyond the ring of pines at the edge of the parking lot. And I began to admire my face in the mirror—the patch still there, the bruised flesh more yellow than purple now.

I was soon back in the groove at the fiberboard plant. The Camaro took me roaring past the dietician's apartment though I couldn't bring myself to ring her buzzer. The guys at work stretched a Welcome Back banner over the forming machine. We all began to hang out at a lounge by the foundry; no one talked about Kate's. And no one mentioned Sonny, though Don and I sometimes cussed him, plotted meanness and revenge with gusto. I began carrying an old Mauser pistol under the seat, one like Peter O'Toole had in *Lawrence of Arabia*.

One Saturday around noon I was buying cases of Coors at the H.E.B. It was fully winter and the day was rain threatening to turn to ice. Someone had rented a cabin up at Lake Bowie and I was to meet a friend of a friend, a girl they said never said no and never got enough. Don and the others had driven on ahead leaving me with the grocery list: beer, more beer, wine, chips.

"You going to speak?"

It was Kate at the near end of the aisle. She was dressed in a colorful Mexican dress with a red scarf around her neck, ready for work at the La Piñata restaurant. She had a cart full of Instant Breakfast, Slender—all powdered things, even the milk.

"Hey, stranger." I walked over, pulling my cart full of beer, and gave her a kiss on the cheek.

We stood and talked. I hadn't seen her in almost a month and Kate loved conversations full of details.

She'd moved back in. She and Lisa had managed to make up.

"Where's Sonny?"

Kate shrugged and told me he'd moved in for two weeks while she'd been living at the trailer. But he didn't have a job and Lisa's trifling money from home wouldn't make it.

"Why don't you two come on up to Bowie?"

Kate grinned the quizzical grin she gave when anyone complimented her. "Gotta work till seven. Lisa's at her parents' this weekend."

But I was feeling tremendous about the girl already up at the cabin and it would be good to have someone along in the Camaro, the stereo blasting. And Kate said she had some good dope. So I talked her into it; it wasn't hard at all.

"Hey," she shouted down the aisle after we parted, "you'll need a key."

"Still got one." I dangled my key ring.

But Kate walked back and took a key out of her clutch purse in the basket. "We changed the locks . . . to keep the asshole out."

"I'll be there when you get off, so hurry up."

She turned away then turned back. "Take a look at the bathroom door."

"What?"

"When you get there, take a look at the door. You'll see Sonny's handiwork. The weapon's in the end table drawer."

"What?"

But Kate liked mystery as well as conversation so she blew me a kiss over her shoulder and walked off, the flounces along her hem not long enough to cover the runners in her dark hose.

I spent the afternoon driving and drinking a lot of the Coors I'd iced down. The Camaro was light in the rear and slipped on the farm road curves. I listened to Dylan and Black Sabbath.

But by five I knew I was getting light-headed and I'd burned almost a half-tank of Shell Extra, so I passed the foundry and drove to Kate's.

Inside I shucked my windbreaker and shirt and toweled off. I made some coffee and turned on the stereo. Even for junior college students they didn't seem to have many books, but I lay on the stained corduroy couch and flipped through some heavy art history text. There was a whole chapter on medieval Christs on the cross. I thought about becoming a Catholic just to see Mother's Primitive Baptist face explode.

I hadn't been back to the apartment since the fight. My eyes drifted past the pages of the book. It was cold and my breath turned to fog. I sat up to retrieve my shirt and looked across the room. The yellow circle of lamplight pitched the bathroom door into relief, its surface pocked and pitted, the white glossy glaze of the paint cracked and split, the yellow pine showing in craters.

I reached over and turned the lamp two clicks higher. Now the room was bright; outside at six o'clock the sky was dark gray.

I walked to the door and ran my hand across the splinters. The damage spread to the facing and even to the wallpaper though its floral pattern partially hid the dozens of gouges.

I pulled on my cold shirt and sat back down on the couch. Then I bent over and opened the drawer, took out the heavy-bladed knife. It was something from the Army, I guessed. The handle leather-covered. It was serious and functional, not a kid's toy for camping trips.

I slid the dull gray blade all the way out of the sheath and stepped over the low coffee table. I took the knife by its tip and slowly drew back, aiming for the undamaged left panel. Then I drew my arm farther back, over my head, and turned slightly to take aim at the already ruined corner.

Three-quarters of the door was a brilliant white. No one I knew could have swung his arm forward to drive the gray tip into the wood. I couldn't imagine how, having done it once and hearing the sound of the damage, he'd thrown it so many times more.

Kate came home later and changed and we drank some beer in the kitchen. She said Allen Lott had promised to help put in a new door; he thought he could fill the places in the facing with wood putty and sand it down. But the wallpaper was the biggest problem.

Later, in the Camaro, Kate laid her head on my leg and slept. The rain still threatened to turn to ice.

The door kept taking me away from myself. I don't think it was pity or sorrow. I didn't know what it was. Standing with the knife over my head I could have been him. But not bringing it forward, I wasn't, I couldn't be. Standing there I was. But throwing the knife crisply into the wood was beyond me. Beyond any of us. It was awful. Three-quarters of the wood white and brilliant. A quarter of it ruined.

I saw Sonny Parker twice that winter before he moved to Corpus Christi. Once he was sitting with a girl at the Pizza Hut. Another time he was alone, walking around the used car lot at the Ford dealership. I would like to say I sat down at their table or that I pulled over to the curb and talked to him about cars, gave him a lift somewhere in the Camaro. But I don't think you should expect too much from a boy, barely twenty, in an East Texas sawmill town in 1973.

Sleet

BILL Powers licked the peanut butter from the crook of his finger and quietly opened the back door. The late October night was cloudless, and bending to look from under the porch's low eaves, he admired the cold brittle starlight.

But he also worried about the advent of the first frost as he padded in his slippers and bathrobe to the far end of the long narrow porch. Here, behind the squat ghostly shape of the deepfreeze, he fumbled for the light switch.

Turning at the click, he watched in delight as the crisscross rows of plastic Japanese lanterns illuminated his garden — brought it instantly out of the moonless shadows to blaze beautifully before him.

The garden, off a hundred feet to his left, behind and beyond the detached garage, was his pride. Since his retirement in late June, gardening had become his occupation. And this garden was unlike any of the others he'd grown over the last thirty years. Those had been just small patches he'd worked at on the few days off from his long-haul trucking job. But this one was immaculate: not a stray blade of grass; well mulched; the rows measured to the inch. The ground around each plant as soft and fine as pastry flour.

For a moment he remembered his first garden at this house. It must have been thirty years ago. Bill smiled at his recollection of Meg carrying heavy buckets of water along the front walk for Carol's struggling flowers and slopping half of it out on herself. No, not Meg. Carol was pregnant with her their first year here.

Bill brought his fingers to his parted lips. It would have to be Sammy. . . he would have been five then. And Carol would be laughing while Sam yelled at his wet clothes in that hoarse voice of his.

Hastily Bill pushed the memory away, as he did all those recollections, and laid it at the end of years of driving and somewhere the other side of Vietnam.

Snapping off the light he watched the garden return to darkness. The weatherman on the ten o'clock news had warned of an approaching front that might bring rain and low temperatures. He'd waited long enough, almost too long, he knew, for the season's last harvest. But the cultivating and trimming and poisoning had replaced forty years of driving that he couldn't exactly say he missed. Most of it was bone-tiring— the wearisome hours, cramped feet and aching spine and the feel of the road along the thighs. But despite all that, it had been the only work he'd ever known. And it was gone now— its cruelty and its only occasional delight.

Standing with his hand on the chilly doorknob, he recalled what had wakened him at 3:00 A.M. and sent him sneaking through the dark house to the refrigerator. In the dream he'd been driving again and the pounding noise of the huge Cummins diesel and the pleasant smells of the wet pavement rushing in through the open window were displaced by low moaning static on his CB. Static unlike the usual banter between truckers concerned with weather and highway patrolmen and where to shop for the cheap speed to help combat the constant dread of falling asleep over the huge steering wheel. No, it was all confusing code words, staccato pieces of sentences; whispered commands or cries for something.

Shaking the dream from his head he opened the door and then latched it behind him. Restless now at an hour that in the past would have found him somewhere else—fighting drowsiness in Colorado or humming along with the slapping windshield wipers in Tennessee—he patrolled the house. He double-checked the doors and windows and passing, finally, down the long hall, the hardwood floor creaking under his heavy weight, he noticed the pale seam of light under the door of Carol's "junk room."

Perplexed, Bill slowly opened the door and reached inside for the light switch. But a low groan and rustle caused him to glance around the door.

Carol's junk room had been Sam's room when he'd lived at home. Before the Army. Now Carol's old sewing machine dominated one corner and rolls of fabric were draped over chairs and footstools and upholstered a short stepladder he'd been missing for months. In another corner her dust-covered exercise bicycle faced a poster of birches she'd tacked to the closet door. In the yellow light he noticed the canceled checks and her lists of chores scattered across her oak desk.

But against the wall opposite the door Carol shifted her weight again and the vinyl of the old sofa crackled under her.

Bill opened his mouth to speak but closed it and crossed over to adjust her blanket that had slipped to the floor. Gently he brought it up to her shoulders and for a moment stood looking down on her feeling the voyeurism one feels watching others sleep.

Turning toward the door he noticed the pictures over a brown, expiring ficus. They were those strange pictures people used to have made years ago where you'd take a photograph and have someone touch up the colors. He guessed they'd been pleased with them at the time, but now the colors weren't quite right. They were too bright and the lines in the faces of Sam and Meg were harsh and outstanding. Bill stood in the middle of the room arrested by them. He hadn't seen either in years; had forgotten they existed at all. And he hadn't seen a picture of Sam for a very long time—certainly not one of him in uniform.

"Billy boy?"

He turned around at the unexpected voice.

Carol lay still, her eyes smiling, the quilt covering her mouth and chin.

"Jesus, Carol."

She pulled her arms from under the covers and tucked her stomach in. She motioned for him to sit in the space she'd cleared, but instead he leaned against the bicycle.

"Handsome boy, huh?" She nodded toward the dim picture.

"Yeah."

"Sit." She patted the couch again. "Let's chat awhile. It's really a thrill to finally have you home after all those years. You don't know how much I've got to catch up on."

"Oh, Carol," Bill sat stiffly on the edge of the sagging couch, "you'd think I'd come home from the war or something."

For a second neither of them spoke. Carol finally sighed and rested her hand on his knee.

"You're doing fine with retirement. . . I know. . . I've been reading some books on it and they all caution. . ."

Bill gently laid his fingers across her mouth and she pretended to bite at them.

"Shhh. . .no library remedies."

Somewhere nearby on the interstate that lay a mile from their driveway, a truck's horn scolded sharply.

"You miss it?" she asked, taking his cold hand from her mouth.

He shrugged. "Sure, some. But listen," and he shifted his weight to bend over her slightly, "since when have you been napping in here?"

Carol grinned and then laughed softly. "Oh, Billy boy,

how little you know about everything at the old homestead. I've slept in here for years." She turned her eyes away from him.

"But you go to bed in your room. I see you."

"And I rest there for a while. Till midnight or so, and then I get up, straighten my rumpled covers and come in here to sew a little or read some."

Disturbed by her revelation, Bill stood and walked toward the door.

"Listen," Carol sat up, the blanket falling and exposing her thin, boy's body in heavy flannel pajamas, "don't go yet. Let's talk, okay? Come on back now."

Bill shook his head and opened the door. "I'm awfully tired."

"How's the garden? It didn't freeze, did it?"

"Nope, not tonight. But tomorrow I'll have to pick everything for sure. There's a cold front moving in."

"I'll help."

"If you want. But I can manage."

"Listen, I've been thinking. . .after the garden's gone, later on in the spring. . .I thought we might take a trip together. You know, to the coast maybe. Just us. It's been a dozen years! The last time was the summer Meg's period suddenly appeared and left her floored for a week. She wouldn't go in, wouldn't do anything but talk proudly about her cramps. Remember? She told the waiter at that place that served the wonderful crab bisque." Carol laid her hands gently across the quilt. "The year Sam graduated."

Bill ran a hand through his thin brown hair. "Maybe we can go down for a couple of days. But I've still got a hell of a lot of things to do. Painting this dark old room for one."

"Oh, say a week, at least a week together. Just us and a fireplace. Hiking through the dunes. Come on, say a week away from carpentry, painting, and fall gardens."

"We'll see." Bill turned the doorknob.

"About Meg," Carol spoke quickly. "I've told her we'd drop over for lunch tomorrow. Okay?"

"Oh, shit." Bill let his shoulders sag and put his head heavily against the door.

"Don't be so theatrical," she laughed softly. "We really do need to see her and the kids. And Bob, too."

"And listen to all their bullshit. Threats. Subtle ugly looks. And he'll be drunker than hell by afternoon. I don't want to deal with all that. And besides," he looked up at her with a smile, "I have to be here to harvest."

"You'll have time—promise."

The house around them was still. Only a few untrimmed branches scraped a wall somewhere.

Carol lay back and fidgeted with the bulky covers. "Do you think they'll divorce someday?"

"Do you sleep with the light on?" His hand rested on the doorknob.

"Sure," she nodded. "Why not? But listen, I could get up and make some coffee and we could bullshit. I'm wide awake now. We could talk about Meg."

Bill shook his head.

"Or about Sam."

He glanced at the pictures but from the door all he could see were the heavy ornate frames full of entangled roses and vines, the depressions chalked with dust.

"What about Sam?"

"Just thought we could recollect together. Bring some of it back."

"Not now. Maybe later." He wished he were out there somewhere, his truck lights tunneling through the dark, the radio pouring out its soul.

"He was a beautiful baby, remember?" Her voice behind him was smooth and calm.

He waved good-night over his shoulder and firmly shut the door behind him. After fumbling his way down the dark hall, he sat on the edge of his damp mattress, the covers flung down between the wall and the bed. The wind blew from the north in increasing gusts and brought with it the sounds of traffic. Bill eased himself back into his bed and lay still. He tried to imagine his room reduced to the comforting close size of a truck's sleeper. There in the dark, parked at a roadside park across a closed service station's driveway, your body soon warms everything near.

They weren't leaving for Meg's until noon, so Bill spent the morning in the garden. And, at the far end of it where he'd left an unplanted spot because of the dense shade of a huge but infertile pear tree, he finally rested from his mindless, captivating labor. He'd brought an old rickety chaise lounge down earlier, after everything had gotten up waist-high, and now he positioned it so that he could watch the house down the rows of tomatoes that hung heavy and red on the dark green stalks.

The weak chair squeaked under his weight and the paper-thin webbing slung his butt only inches from the loose soil. Idly, he inspected his dirty coveralls. Carol had ripped off the company logo over one pocket and his safe-driving patch — "Twenty Year Trucker," it had said — from his left sleeve. Only his name showed over his grimy left pocket.

Bill gave up more of his weight and sank back to close his eyes. The wind rustled his plants, and the weak sunlight through the pear tree spotted his face and forced him to turn his head to one side. He enjoyed the tiredness of his big body. His calves ached from the squatting and his neck was already sore to the touch.

Every day since his retirement had been like this: full of exhausting work; hours almost as long and busy as his truck driving had been. Up early and hard at staking, spraying, mowing, and painting until he lumbered into bed at eight or nine.

"Bill . . . lunch."

Involuntarily he slumped in the chair, forced himself deep into its weak net. Down the row he could just barely make out her face as she stood with the screen door open. He watched Carol carefully searching the garden and then the yard.

"Bill? Billy boy?"

He didn't want to go in yet. He didn't want to go to Meg's. And he never wanted to hear Sam's name again so easily off her tongue. All the hell he wanted was to stay right here and work all day getting his vegetables in.

"Bill, dammit, answer me!" Her voice was full of concern now and he could tell she had started around to the front yard.

Moving slowly he crawled out of the chaise lounge and carefully worked his way to the garden fence. On his knees, he pushed back some of the thick tangle of blackberry vines and watched her disappear around the corner of the rambling white frame house.

He squeezed his eyes shut and there was the silence of his truck cab; the comfortable bass hum of the heavy tires. All around him the altering landscape. Behind him somewhere his family, his house, everything else. All of it somehow connected by the maze of a million miles of asphalt and concrete. Filtered by the vacuum at his trailer's end and the roar of air slicing off his hood. Diluted by all the rain and road crews and flagmen and motels and midnight coffee in between. If there was trouble or unhappiness or pain, what better than this hurtling somewhere at ninety with thirty-five tons of load behind you, your lights carving day out of night.

Rubbing his eyes, he rose feeling silly for his child's game of hide-and-seek and walked to the gate. Far down the lane leading to the highway, he heard her call his name. It drifted back through the trees.

All afternoon low, bruised clouds had hurried down from the north and now, as Bill and Carol waved good-bye to Meg and the children and backed out of the drive, rain began to fall and the temperature began to drop.

Bill, worried about his garden, sped home using a crumbly asphalt back road. But only a few miles from their house, the car plowed through a huge pothole and the engine died immediately.

"Aw, shit." Bill tugged hard at the wheel, its power steering gone, until he had forced the heavy Buick onto the narrow shoulder. The red lights on the dash glared and the wipers and radio continued their noise.

Carol grinned and reached across the long bench seat to pat his shoulder. "So, a shortcut, huh?" Her voice was low and soft. "What now, Billy boy?"

Bill turned the key again and again but the starter ground uselessly. The red lights blinked. "Distributor's soaked. I'll have to dry it off somehow." He zipped up his heavy windbreaker.

They both looked out the windshield, now covered by a flowing sheet of water. Rain pounded the roof. All around them the rain distorted the scenery—bloating the nearby trees, ludicrously emaciating the dark road that disappeared a few yards ahead around a curve.

"You'll drown out there. Let's just wait awhile and then I'll help."

"How?" Again he tried the engine but now the old battery skipped a beat, the starter wore down to a lower growl. Despite the chill, he felt sweat run down his temples.

"Oh, I'll hold a newspaper over your head." Carol settled

in the seat and drew her light jacket around her. She looked out her window at the woods.

Bill turned the key back and reached over to adjust the radio. He knew it wouldn't drain off enough power to matter.

The rain swept in sheets now and occasionally he could feel the wind gust up under the car and rock it gently on its tires. Bits and pieces of words and static interrupted the sound of the rain. Unusual noise because of the weather. Low hums and brutal high whines. Fragments of words as imperative as commands forced themselves into the gray-green light of the car.

Finally he found some football game and sat listening to its meaningless chatter. The road, which cut across one end of a state forest, was empty this late on a Sunday afternoon full of wind and rain.

Slowly the windows clouded over with fog. Carol, her head averted, sighed deeply and reached up to brush clear a circle.

Bill felt the windshield with the back of his hand and wondered how cold it was now. He needed to get home before it began freezing and ruined most of his garden.

"So you didn't know about my secret?"

"What?"

"My sleeping in Sammy's room. You never knew that?"

"No, why should I?" Bill rubbed his face anxiously and tried again, his thumb turning white as he twisted the key. But the growl was even weaker. He switched off the radio.

"It wasn't at all like this when we buried him, was it?" Still looking out the window, carefully touching up her small circle, she continued as if he'd answered. "The sun was almost too bright. It threw everything into sharp detail—blues and greens. And remember, they'd covered the mound of dirt with Astroturf." Carol laughed softly, her breath fogging now in the cold air. "It's funny how what remains years later isn't any of what was going on then. God, a million scraps of things flooded my head. And look what's left."

Bill tried the engine. But now the weak battery groaned and rested and groaned again.

"Well, shit." He thumped the steering wheel with his fist. "What now?"

He shrugged and tapped his fingers on the dash.

"What were you thinking?"

"Huh?" He jerked his head off the cold vinyl headrest and glanced at Carol. The dim light seemed to accent the crow's-feet above the corners of her mouth. She had turned in the seat and was resting her head against the glass; her feet brushed his pants leg.

"When we buried Sammy. During all that military hoopla—rifle shots and folded flags. What were you thinking?"

He fingered the dangling keys. "I don't know. What you were thinking, I guess. About all the military business. . . that. . .and everything else, too."

Carol bent toward him a little. "Why didn't you kiss him?"

Bill swung around startled. "What?"

"At the funeral home. When we first went by. That Saturday after they'd brought him in. I went by first and then you. You bent down low and pursed your lips but you stopped an inch from his forehead. Remember? Don't you remember why?"

"Good God, Carol, that was years ago." The rain distracted him for a moment. He listened for the tap of sleet. "I thought I did. . .had. . .I'm sure I must have." He stared at her, his mouth open.

A single car whooshed by on the road, tossing gravel and water against the car. Bill quickly reached down to flick his lights on and off but the car had swung around the curve.

"Fifteen years, Billy boy. Fifteen goddamned years, Billy boy, and how much have we talked about it? Three times? Four?" Her voice was dull and low.

Slowly, he moved his hand to the door handle near his knee.

"I'm left to thrash about on my bed, alone, until finally one night—after gaining twenty pounds from camping in front of the refrigerator—I sleep there. In the middle of it all. Before we moved a single thing out I was already there." She gulped for air. "And there's Meg."

Bill's hand forced the lever down and the door opened an inch. "Listen, we need to get home. I've got to get back to the garden before it freezes." Suddenly he stood and closed the door behind him. The rain was frigid and constant and soaked him where he stood, his hand still on the outside handle.

Carol brought her face close to the windshield, her hands spread on the wide dash. He watched her eyes widen and her mouth move as she spoke. She reached out and touched the glass, but he turned and started down the road toward town.

Behind him Carol honked the horn—it moaned like a cow—but he didn't glance back.

Around the curve the horn was muffled by the wind and rattle of rain in the trees.

He stopped and stood looking down into the muddy swirling water that erupted in brown foam from a small culvert. His head felt as if it were filled by the rush of wind and the cold spattering rain. He walked back towards the car, then stopped and turned. Again at the culvert he halted and put his hands to his ears, hoping to shut out everything. But the high wind tossed the branches and the water smacked the pavement at his feet.

Bill turned and ran. His heavy body fought the unexpected motion—his huge, woman's breasts swung down hard and painful against his ribs, the weak muscles instantly stretched and strained. His bulging gut spilled over his belt and rolled free.

The water streamed in his face, smeared his vision, confined his sight to the dark shapes of the trees and the light gray of the clouds.

His clothes, soaked and twisted by his heaving body, choked his movement. Looking down at his feet he watched his dress shoes swell and spread as they filled with rainwater and pounded the rough uneven surface of the road.

At first he lumbered down the edge of the road, struggling to keep his balance, oblivious to everything but the surprise of his movement.

Then, the noise in his head dying out, he moved onto the middle of the road away from the cracks and potholes along its edge. And he ran.

He forced it all to recede as easily as the final shift into the highest gear. Now he was pulling hard up a hill. Then he was coasting down the other side as easily as ice on glass. Effortlessly. And each rushing line was further protection. A charm against all the world.

After awhile his heart pounded and his side stitched a constant pain. And even though he slowed his speed, he kept his eye on the yellow stripes.

Meg's husband was a drunk who beat her with his fists. Sammy died on a Friday morning in Hue. He shook the thoughts out. Ran beyond them. Outdistanced them all.

Finally a shoe flung off into the dark and brought him abruptly to a limp. Moving back to the deteriorated edge of the old road he hobbled past the bypass that led into town and turned into their driveway where the rain became mixed with sleet and rattled past the few tenacious dead leaves. It stung the back of his neck like nettles.

He took down the spare key from over the door and let himself in. The phone was ringing loud and insistent on the far end of the kitchen counter. Automatically he moved toward it, his hand outstretched, but he knew who it was and he didn't answer.

It rang and didn't stop. But over its racket a gust of wind threw a handful of sleet against the windowpanes.

"The garden," he said, and shoved open the door and loped across the soggy yard to the fence.

The sleet lay solid and unmelting on the ground. And already the water on the tomato leaves and herbs had begun to freeze. The late peppers were thinly glazed. The icy leaves of the basil and tarragon plants had bent the bushes to the wet earth.

He hurried down the rows, his big hands fumbling to pick everything at once, his bare foot sliding and sucking in the mud. But he only had his shirttail for a basket, and with the increasing cold and heavier downpour of sleet and rain, he finally opened his hands and let it all scatter at his feet.

Over Bill's head the dark shapes of the Japanese lanterns fluttered against the gray sky like a surprised flock of birds.

Field of Vision

"WELL, when *will* we 'think about it'?" Beth threw the words back at him across the cracked vinyl upholstery of the car seat and avoided his eyes by concentrating on the distant black specks that were buzzards.

Richard sighed dramatically and without a hint of resignation. "Like I said, soon. We just can't afford it now. That's all."

Even against the clutter of her thoughts she began earnestly to study the wind-blown birds. To examine the perspective, judge the technique required to draw them there, so far off. So unimpeded by things. She had always wanted to draw them but never seemed to find the time. "It's going to be awful," she said. "Absolute hell in the kitchen during the summer. And mildew this winter. Remember how it ruined my shoes?" She almost let her voice crack in front of him but held it steady. She despised how her anger often took the form of tears. His seldom caused his voice to rise, much less falter. She clenched the torn and faded armrest. "We don't seem able to afford anything, do we?"

Richard shrugged and leaned over to turn off the sputtering car engine. "Maybe when we get it sealed properly and all the insulation in. Then maybe we can talk about something cooler than fans and warmer than space heaters. Maybe next spring." He turned his head and looked out the car window toward the house.

His movement took her away from the cool blue sky of the buzzards to look with him past their mailbox and across the wooded valley no more than two hundred yards wide. Only a portion of his handbuilt A-frame house showed through the young pines and older but smaller post oaks.

There was the yellow gleam of a window already reflecting the steadily mounting light of the morning sun—the windows themselves he had salvaged from the demolition of an old schoolhouse in a nearby town. The flat, deep-red siding he had loaded himself at a mill halfway across the state. Anything he hadn't been able to get secondhand, he had haggled over for weeks—in person or on the phone—until the salesman had finally sold more out of exasperation and the desire never to see him again than from a sense of having reached an equitable price. He seldom bought materials from the same source more than once.

Already the morning heat stirred the flies that minutes earlier had hovered lethargically near the sun visor.

Beth turned on the worn seat and reached back to retrieve the manila envelope. "You've got everything? Lunch? Cap?"

"Of course."

She patted his hand. The hair along its back like the finest golden thread was turning, under the roofer's scalding sun, to white. It's strange, she thought, that his pale skin neither tanned nor burned.

"Off you go then." She opened the door and came around to stand between him and the house. She tapped the envelope. "Who knows? Maybe this'll bring thousands." And she smiled.

Richard grunted and looked up at her as she bent down and touched her lips to his forehead. Her thick tangled hair—gypsy's hair he had once called it—filled the window.

"Stay cool."

He smiled slightly, the corners of his thin lips puckered. "I'll try. You weed the garden." And he shook an admonitory finger at her—more in seriousness, they both knew, than in jest.

And then he was gone. The red dust of the road, like dust from pulverized bricks, swirled behind the rattling Toyota, and she stood still long enough to watch some of it settle another layer on the Spanish mulberries, the waxy leaves of poison ivy along the roadside. What remained aloft, the first warm morning breeze guided cautiously between the scaly trunks of the pines.

For a moment she forgot about him and the humidity and the heat of their second summer in the unfinished house and thought only about the half-dozen pen-and-ink sketches she was sending to an art magazine. They were the best she had ever drawn. Especially the one of Jackie's boy, Neal. In her drawing the child's face was hidden. All you saw was his naked back and legs—the two-year-old fat on his thighs, spilling over his knees. Beth had wanted a child for years, but Richard had never seemed ready to discuss the possibility seriously. Something new always intervened. Only six months ago he'd used the house as his excuse.

"It's not built for children, is it?" he'd said.

"Why not?"

"Well, Christ! Look around. We have a loft for a bedroom. A ladder to it. No stairs yet. Books everywhere. No yard to speak of."

"But when, then?"

"When we're settled in more. When we get a little ahead. When we can build a nursery. That's what we both wanted, isn't it?"

With the back of her hand, Beth wiped a line of water from her forehead, then walked to the silver mailbox. She bent the envelope, careful to keep it curved as she slid it in. The red flag, as she raised it, was warm against her fingertips.

On her way back to the house, down the deeply rutted road that lacked a bar ditch and turned into a shallow stream with every rain, she stopped at the garden. She guessed she'd better follow his orders; the weeds were overshadowing the smaller plants. She walked carefully past the knee-high corn— its green dramatic in contrast to the red powdery earth—and the hills of young cucumbers whose pale yellow blooms were just beginning to show, pulled up her pants leg, and squatted by the carrots. She gathered her hair and tied it in a wiry ball behind her ears with a rubber band from her shirt pocket. Methodically, she began to weed—trying patiently to distinguish between actual weeds and the tiny first filigree of the carrot tops. Soon she had to rest her elbows on the ground, her butt in the air. She inched her way down the row, crawling forward, careful to keep her body compact, her legs and feet exactly between the rows.

"Shit." She finally straightened—the muscles in her forearms and along her sides aching. She held an almost invisible weed up to the pale blue of the sky and began to doubt herself. "Goddammit, it's a carrot." She looked back at her five or six feet of weeding and realized that she had taken as many carrot seedlings out as she had weeds.

It's *his* garden anyway, she thought angrily and stood, slowly trying the taut muscles. His methodical handiwork surrounded her: the critically measured distances between the rows; the tomato stakes all the same height; the cotton twine that not only laid out the perimeter of the field but also internally laid out the individual rows.

A gust of wind caused the symmetrical white twine to undulate gently like the strands of a spider's web, and Beth felt trapped in the carefully woven garden like some clumsy insect.

All through the morning she worked for him, as she thought of it. She performed her chores as if he were right there, looking over her shoulder. Before, she had been comforted by his presence. But now he made her nervous. And the steadily increasing heat seemed to pique their earlier argument. The hotter it became the slower she worked and the more aggravating each task was to perform. She became awkward and careless. She salted the stew too heavily, and mindful of what his comments would have been, she dumped it far behind the house in a small hollow under some pines. Ashamed, she pulled some leaves over it with the toe of her shoe. And, inside again, she swept the floor, but almost as if to irritate him, she swept carelessly around the legs of the furniture.

Even the cat, which she loved because of its companionship, caused her worry. The tenth time it wailed to be let out to empty its weak bladder, she took a solid swipe at it with the broom. The dirty yellow bobtailed cat screamed at the mistreatment and scrambled hard to catch the boards at the porch's edge. But snared by her anger, Beth stepped through the opened screen and took a harder, more purposeful swing.

"Oh God," she called after the cat. "Sarah. Sarah." She felt tears fill her eyes. But she bit her lip hard and thought of something else. She half-turned to enter the house but paused to run her hand gently over the smooth unstained wood of the porch railing that was taking on the color of chocolate. She remembered having asked him to leave it rough because she enjoyed the prickle of it against her fingers. And she recalled his tight, controlled laugh—the force of it cut short—at her suggestion. And then she had agreed with him, had laughed at herself. For a few moments she stroked the sanded wood and stood listening to the rustle of the yellow cat's retreat through the undergrowth.

What would I do with a child underfoot in this heat? she wondered as she continued sweeping. If I can't tolerate an old cat, what would a baby be like? But she had an answer for herself: That would be different. And a nice change from the impersonal attention of the old cat. Then chores wouldn't be his and mine. I could work for both of us through the child. He'd have to be kept entertained — crayons brought out and scissors supervised. I'd have to watch him carefully as he played in the bare spots under the spindly post oaks.

Imagining her life with a child helped relieve the tedium of the chores for a while, but by three o'clock she had to surrender to the heat and her increasing frustration. Any movement, no matter how short-lived, produced a torrent of perspiration.

She sat heavily in a rocking chair as motionless as an insect pinned on a card and watched, through the upper windowpanes of old warped glass, a flight of buzzards far off. They meandered amidst the updrafts of woodsair, the glass elongating them suddenly, then as quickly causing them to disappear. They were swallowed up from both ends, disappearing into themselves.

She wanted a better view, a closer look at those ugly birds that searched for lifeless carrion, the smashed bodies of raccoons and skunks and occasionally dogs and tabby cats that lay beside the roads. She remembered her father's surveying equipment that she had carefully packed and moved through her life since his death fifteen years ago. She felt that if she could get a good look at the buzzards, a closer look, then she would be able to draw them. She climbed the ladder against the far wall between the couch and the stereo, her feet and hands secure on the smooth rungs.

Upstairs in the loft the fuzzy synthetic bedspread looked scorching. The air was so stifling she panted for breath and lunged across the narrow room to push up the aluminum windows. But now there was the faintest breeze, and the hot still air of the room was slowly discharged and replaced by the slightly cooler outside air.

She lay flat and looked up under the bed, afraid of mice

or other small animals that had lived with them since they had erected this place and interrupted trails, burrows, and territories.

The boxes lay pushed against the farthest wall and she had to thrust herself half under the bed to reach them. Her tangled hair caught in the underside of the open springs and for a moment she panicked, felt the dark closeness of the dirty air and heard the scratching of mice. She yanked back vehemently and sacrificed a few strands.

She pawed the boxes out into the open and sat up, two dirty circles on her shirt where her breasts had mopped up the dust.

Cautiously she emptied the contents, still wary of spiders, of anything that might rush out suddenly.

Her mother had left little behind. Except for the now odorless sachets she'd taken from her mother's dresser drawers, and the small velvet boxes of ancient, mismatched earrings and out-of-fashion pendants—a yellow cameo chipped beyond recognition—there was nothing. But here were tools a person could use, if she knew how to read the contents of these boxes and to figure their secrets. She opened a box of small yellow fieldbooks and turned to a page full of numbers and symbols many of which were foreign and indecipherable.

"Boundary Surveys," it read in block letters. And along the top border, in small script, the names of the crew members: her father's first as party chief. The weather: cool, 65 degrees, partly cloudy. Finally, the date. She looked up through the window absentmindedly and figured. He had been thirty then. No, thirty-two.

She turned quickly through the pages, passing through his work days. The lingering coolness of late spring. The brief and rare snowfall. Lot surveys. Boundary surveys. At the back of the book, behind the tables of logarithms, charts on how to figure grades and how to calculate chords from deltas and radii, were pages filled with penciled additions and subtractions. She closed the book, recognizing the awkward figures of his 2s and 4s.

But all of this wasn't what she was after. She brusquely shoved the fragile old books back under the bed and wiped her forehead. A longer cardboard box, crushed at both ends, yielded the tools themselves. She remembered enough to recognize the long wooden box of the level. The varnish was eaten away in places, and where the wood had been exposed, mildew clouded the surface, softening it to a damp sponginess. Hadn't she warned him about mildew just this morning? She ran her hand gently across the ruined wood and, remembering her original intent, looked out the raised windows to the distant ridge beyond their own small valley. Even though it was only a few miles away, on days like today she imagined those distances cool and windy.

Carefully she opened the level case and lifted out the heavy tube. She ran her hands along the warm screws and indentations for adjustments and fine tuning that she didn't fully understand, then crawled across the bed, gently dragging the level behind her. There was just enough space between the bed and window for her to kneel, the level's base on the windowsill.

For a while, as she tried to adjust the knobs—turning screws one way and then the other, rotating rings around the eyepiece left and right—pine needles leapt at her only to retreat, and scaly pine bark was clear one second only to dissolve into an indistinct blur of gray-green.

But finally, after stacking a half-dozen fieldbooks under the base, she had managed to tilt the telescope above and beyond the short pines and oaks of their valley and towards the hills in the distance.

She kept looking with one eye and then the other. And once she had her left eye—her best without her glasses—to the barrel, she slowly swept the flanks of the ridge. What to her naked eyes was only a green wall became separate trees. Huge pines clung to the slopes too steep for logging. And the scattered oaks were draped in the curly tufts of Spanish moss.

Suddenly something streaked across her narrow field of vision and when it crossed again she jerked the level around with it. But in her hands the tube bobbed violently no matter how rigid she tried to keep her arms. She fought the same anger she had felt toward the cat and continued to sweep up from the ridge and into the deep blue of the later afternoon sky. And it was as if she had never seen it before. As if she had parted the hot hazy air with the level, had cut visually through the breath of the woods, through the wet exhalations all around her. She pressed her shoulder hard into the windowframe.

Once again there were buzzards high over the ridge — they were what had blurred across her small circle. She tried to keep them in the thin cross hairs but either they bobbed and floated too quickly on the currents or else she was too unsteady. Whatever the reason, she couldn't keep them in sight. They drifted across at their own speed unaffected by her desire to hold them still, to make them flow with and match her own movements.

"Goddamn you." Her voice was hoarse, but she kept muttering. "Just let me see. I need to draw you." But the huge birds wouldn't cooperate and so she rested the level back on the pile of books. Her eyes stung, strained by the magnification. She rubbed them with her knuckles and took up the sweep of the distance again.

She was oblivious to the heat of the room, to the time, to the smell of the new pot of stew drifting up the ladder well.

Farther along the ridge to the northeast she found the dim silver wedge of the waning moon. And she breathed in shallowly as she fumbled with the focus on the side of the tube. She had never seen it like this before — the shadow eating it away, a gradually darkening ring. The craters deep and in shadows. The face of it pitted and awesome. She had seen relief maps and photographs but she had never seen for herself.

She kept looking from the instrument to see it with both eyes. But to her eyes, shaded from the weak late-afternoon light by the eaves, the sliver appeared smooth and bland and usual.

She had the desire to turn and drop down the ladder to her sketchpad, then to rush back up to their bed and draw what she had seen for the first time: the ridge both a wall of shades of green and yet individual trees; the indistinct blur of black curiously at ease with the cobalt sky; the rough face of the waning moon. But instead she scanned it all again, having already ritualized her sweep: from the dark ridge to the few remaining buzzards that hadn't dropped down to roost for the night to the rising piece of moon.

It seemed only a matter of minutes before the rusted yellow Toyota drifted noiselessly into the faint cross hairs. When it reached their driveway, she realized that Richard must have switched off the engine. She glanced away from the eyepiece to her watch—he was early.

The car slowed and came to rest on the small stone bridge, and Richard emerged in his dirty work clothes—the shirt dark with perspiration, the pants splotched with tar and oil from the shingles.

She warmed to this game. Certainly she had observed him from across the room at parties—had watched him lean belligerently against a far wall, or, more rarely, had seen his tailored smile and heard him laugh, his voice slightly false to her ears. But this was new and exciting. Here he was alone. She gladly followed him from the car, back up the hill, to where a path cut through the trees to the garden.

But the quickly failing light made it more difficult for

her to find him between the intervening trees. Anxiously she bounded across the chenille bedspread and opened the square box. The heavier transit—shorter and thicker of body—was higher in magnification. She remembered this from her father at a distance of more than two dozen years.

At the window she tried to focus quickly, worried at having lost sight of him for so long—of having missed any second of this rare opportunity. She fumbled with the knobs. Her hands were sweaty and her fingers slid off the warm metal. She heard herself breathe in and felt her lungs catch for a fraction of a second as she brought his face to within an arm's reach.

Just as quickly as she had begun, she now wanted to end this spying. To lower the aluminum windows and crawl back across their rumpled bed, seal up the boxes and leave these instruments alone for the mice and mildew. She felt shameful like some child caught in a dirty act by the sudden opening of a door.

But she ignored this part of herself because, under the stronger magnification, the pale face drew her on. And for the first time in almost eight years of marriage, she thought she saw the truth in his face across the distance of a few hundred yards—the meanness in his blond eyebrows, the ugliness congealed in the tight set of his fleshless lips.

She turned away for a moment to rub at her watering eyes and when she turned back to the transit he was gone. She scanned the patches of garden she could see—the bright stalks of corn, the wire pens for the cucumbers. But he had drifted silently from her field of vision.

With an artificial calm she swept the valley before her as she had learned to scan the hills earlier. But still she had no luck and in the twilight the trees seemed to be absorbing the last stray particles of light.

She muttered to herself. Out of desperation she began at the car, and as she traversed slowly to the left, she saw him emerge from the path and walk toward the creek.

She watched him jump down into the dry ditch by the side of the car. She tried to sharpen her focus but in the darkness she could only intimate some things.

She knew that he removed a stone from the tight-fitting headwall he had built to keep the rains from eating at the road where the creek crossed it. And she saw him reach into the opening — the white luminescent hand was swallowed up — to remove a pouch like the sandwich bags she packed his lunch in. And his hand moved again, from his shirt pocket to the bag. Then the bag and rock back in place.

And for the second time she saw his face clearly. This time he almost jerked his head up toward the house and seemed to look directly into her eyes. His thin blond hair was ruffled by some breeze down there that failed to touch her higher up the hill. The heat around her was still as thick and palpable as a shawl.

It seemed as if they watched one another for a long time. And in that time she tried to interpret his face a hundred different ways.

Even after she heard the whine of the starter and the crunch of the gravel on the drive, she still held her eye to her father's transit and continued to watch the blurred dark circle of road that ran across the dry creek.

Recovering, she meticulously smoothed the crumpled bedcovers and carefully repacked the tools. Then she pushed them back into the dust under the bed.

Once downstairs she bent over the simmering stew and stabbed at it with a wooden spoon. It had been money, she told herself. That had to be what he had folded and placed behind the stone.

"Hello," Richard said. He had stopped on the porch to remove his filthy boots.

Beth turned, the spoon still in her hand, dripping brown

gravy on the stovetop and her blouse. "I'm pregnant," she enunciated, her voice unfaltering.

"What?" He had bent over at the waist to untie his shoes and now he turned his white face upward to see her.

"I'm *pregnant*." This time she spewed the words at him, and she knew that if she really wasn't, then very soon she would be.

PHILIP'S eyes opened at the touch and he saw high bright green hills a dozen yards from the plane's wing tips. For a second he thought they were crashing and his hand shot out to Mike's empty seat. Turning his head, he glared past the stewardess's close, forced smile, frantically looking for his son.

"I'm sorry I startled you," the stewardess said. Her hand still rested on his shoulder. Her English was partially strangled by her Spanish accent. Her tongue pried at the syllables. "You need to bring your seat forward. We'll be landing soon."

"My son . . . Mike . . . he was right here a minute ago."

She nodded and smiled, her teeth large and straight. "He's near the rear. Found himself a window seat for the landing." She waved a thin graceful arm. "Right back there."

Philip nodded and started to fasten the belt across his lap. Christ, he thought, and sighed deeply. The whole purpose of the trip was to catch up on things. They had a whole year's worth of things to talk about, and all he'd managed to do was doze off. Good work, Philip, he told himself as he dropped the seat belt and stood in the aisle.

The plane was almost full. Many people were smoking and reading newspapers and magazines in Spanish. Businessmen talked and drank steadily. He walked stiffly back toward the restroom and, almost there, he saw Mike sitting alone, his face touching the plexiglass. As he sat by him he noted

127

once again how much Mike had changed in the last year. How different this young man was from the idle, slack-jawed child he had dropped off at his mother's apartment a year ago. Sheridan Academy had certainly turned him around.

"Hey." Philip patted his son's shoulder.

Mike turned and regarded his father for a moment.

Self-consciously Philip ran his hands over his face and then through his tousled hair. "Just woke up. Not much sleep last night—all the packing and last-minute stuff. Sorry I dozed off. We're almost there, huh?" He looked past the boy to the mountains. Despite the gray afternoon he could detect individual palms and other trees outlined on the low hilltops. In the valley below, a river gleamed like a pewter ribbon.

"Ready to sail? It's been a long time since we did. When was it? Remember?"

The boy's fingers idly flipped through the magazines crammed in the pocket at his knee. "We were with the Petersens. Mom went too." His fingers stopped and he pulled out a tattered copy of the airline's magazine. On its cover Honduran dancers were frozen in some ancient frenzy of swirling colors and smoke from pots of incense near their feet. Mike glanced at his father. "Two years ago on Canyon Lake. You were trying to teach me anchoring drill."

Philip nodded and stood to stuff his shirt back into his pants. The boy seemed suddenly occupied with the magazine. But Philip felt an urgent need to talk with him. They had a million things to catch up on, but somehow he couldn't find a single thing to talk about.

"They tell me the sailing here's like the British Virgins were fifty years ago." His words rushed out. "And the snorkeling...that's something else...one of the ten best places in the world...only the finest, huh?" Philip reached out and touched the boy's close-cropped hair. It was dry and cool to his fingers.

Mike pulled away and looked up with a smile. "Dad, don't do that, okay?"

Philip leaned awkwardly against the empty seat in front of him. "But you say the Academy doesn't have sailing? I was sure it was in the catalogue." He grinned. "What're you taking for an activity?"

Mike shook his head and smiled. "For the third time... marksmanship this year and skeet next semester."

"Your grandfather was a helluva shot. I never cared for it... but you'll do just fine."

"Dad..." Mike gestured with his magazine and Philip turned to see one of the stewardesses motion for him to sit.

"Need to pee," he mumbled to Mike and walked to the back of the plane. With his hand on the door, he stopped and turned back toward his son. He noticed Mike's cropped hair again, as he had several times since Karen had brought him to the airport. He wondered if she'd been upset the first time she'd seen him. He remembered how much she had loved his fine long hair.

She'd loved all sorts of awful things about him. She'd encouraged his foolishness and girlfriends. And, indirectly, his dope smoking and late hours. For six months the two of them would buddy together and talk like teenagers. Then he'd have hell with him for six months. Clothes everywhere. Nothing but smart-assed talk. Absolutely no volition. Hours of MTV. He'd seen all he'd hoped for cascade down around them during terrible battles everywhere and at any time. Rages at Mike's grandparents' house. On Karen's doorsteps. Weeping and cursing. The boy stalking off in the middle of the night to stay at some friend's house. And those friends...! Philip shook his head and rocked gently as the airplane turned, following the valley.

But his arrest for marijuana had changed all that. It had awakened Karen from her careless world for a moment. He

winced as he thought of her and her friends and her apartment full of her "art," as she so glibly called it. Tapestries woven
from odds and ends. Crushed beer cans included at random
places in the pattern.

"Excuse me, sir." A short fat man pushed past Philip and
slid into the other restroom.

Philip watched his son return the magazine to the pocket
and resume his gaze out the window. Surely she'd cried when
Mike mailed her his first pictures. He knew she phoned him
every Sunday night, when they were permitted to take calls.
But she must be proud of him now. The people at the Academy
had done what the rest of them couldn't—not him or her or
grandparents. Sometimes he almost broke out in a sweat when
he thought how close they had come to losing the boy. Losing
him to dope, idleness, and bad friends. After Mike had sent
home those first pictures of himself in uniform, he'd decided
that next year he was going to use his vacation from designing
supermarkets to write an article or two for the local paper
on the awful public school system. Thank God, he could afford
an alternative.

Still, as he lifted the lid to urinate, he wondered what
Mike had looked like sitting ramrod straight on the edge of
her couch surrounded by the riot of wall hangings. And what
in God's name had they talked about?

They were supposed to leave for the island the next
morning—just a short hop of thirty minutes over the last wall
of mountains to the coast and beyond it fifty miles—so after
breakfast Mike used his Spanish to ask the desk clerk when
they should leave for the airport.

"What's he say?" Philip asked, wiping a fleck of egg off
his shirt.

Mike gestured for his father to be quiet and continued
talking.

Idly Philip turned away and rambled through the cavernous lobby of the expensive hotel. On one side a shop sold native crafts: chunky, squat pottery, intricately woven blankets, acrylics by local artists. One held his attention. It was an unbelievably crowded canvas, jammed with brown faces. Mouths opened in perfect ovals, far down the throats the red hint of the uvula. A hundred dark eyes speckled with gold. Somehow it didn't seem the right painting for a hotel shop.

"Bad news."

"Huh?" Philip didn't turn from the painting.

"Weather's awful in the bay. And no lights or radar at the field. What sorta place you get me into anyway?"

Philip turned to his son. The boy's face, his forehead level with Philip's eyes, was set in a thin smile. "Your Spanish is great. Really sounds fine. You'll take it next year. . .?"

"Sure. It's the most practical."

"Well, what do we do now?"

Mike was looking over Philip's shoulder at the things in the window. "Look at all that junk."

Philip turned back and rested his hand on the boy's shoulder. "What junk?" he laughed.

"That picture for one. Looks like those syrupy big-eyed kids."

"Well. . ."

"And those things." His finger brushed the glass.

Philip felt the stiff cloth of his son's shirt and for a moment wanted to clasp the boy's shoulder as hard as he could.

"They're like that stuff Mom hangs on her walls." Mike grinned and shook his head. "Except no cans or bottles. Bet they're returnable here."

Philip nodded but at the same time felt some strange allegiance to Karen. "Now, now, her stuff's not that bad."

They stood in silence for a minute.

"Let's walk. Explore this place. What do you say?"

Mike shrugged. "If you say so."

Together they walked down the gravel driveway of the hotel and beyond its quiet grounds to the busy street at the bottom of the hill.

Here the city was a rampage of noise and traffic. On every street corner were two or three soldiers in camouflage fatigues, their pants blossoming over heavy boots.

"Jesus, look at that." Mike stopped at the side of one young soldier who eyed them suspiciously until Mike spoke his perfect Spanish.

Philip bent over a newspaper rack and tried to read the headlines but couldn't. Bending closer he noticed the photos. There was a jumble of elbows and feet. The flat black of blood in wirephotos. More a hole in the pavement near the shattered head than a pool on it. He quickly jerked straight and motioned for Mike to come on.

"Okay, what's so interesting?"

"He's a veritable Whitman sampler of the arms market. Israeli machine gun. Our old army fatigues. French pistol. Wow." Mike's face was bright with excitement.

They finally dodged their way across the street and turned downhill. Mixed with the flat oily smell of diesel was the sharp odor of sewage.

"Yuck . . . smells good." Mike clamped his nose dramatically with a thumb and forefinger.

"I didn't know you were so hot on guns."

"Weapons. That's what we call them."

"Whatever. I didn't know you cared for all that."

Mike shrugged. "Dad, it's something we fool with a lot. You just pick it up, that's all." The boy seemed to pull himself in a bit, to shrink into his immaculate shirt.

Philip remembered when he had bought a gun, the only one he had ever owned. He and Karen had just married and they were living in Houston. She worked until ten at night teaching weaving to adults at Clear Lake Community College. And one night he had taken the pistol from their bureau to clean it and managed to shoot a chunk out of their hardwood floor. Lights in the apartment complex had gone on. People had rushed out into the hall. Dogs had howled. He'd covered the hole with a dab of plastic wood and brown shoe polish and given the pistol, next Christmas, to his father, who'd turned it in his large hand and smiled at its small caliber. No, he couldn't talk guns, weapons, with Mike. And try as hard as he could, he simply couldn't picture the boy prone behind a green wall of sandbags on a practice range.

The street became more narrow and soon they were picking their way, with everyone else, around buckled slabs of concrete and crimson puddles. Here there were no soldiers at all—there was nothing worth protecting. Cinder blocks lay scattered everywhere and whole neighborhoods were jumbles of half-finished walls and luxurious wreaths of creepers. Emaciated dogs sprawled underfoot, angular sacks of bones, as if all their stuffing had suddenly escaped. Philip couldn't tell, not even with a gentle prod of his shoe, if they were alive or not.

And despite its being only a couple of days from Christmas, the humidity and heat were enervating. Often Philip stopped in one of the shops that seemed stocked with only a few packs of cigarettes and a neat pyramid of votive candles and bought a beer which he gulped down in hard swallows. Mike always shook his head at the offer. In one shop Philip bought a pack of the harsh local cigarettes and lit the first he'd had in almost eighteen months.

He inhaled deeply and let the boy walk ahead a dozen feet. Several times he almost called to him to show him something interesting in one of the shop windows. His head floated from the beer and strong cigarettes. He knew he needed to talk, to re-establish contact with his son. Sweat soaked his light shirt, wilted the crease in his white pants. He wiped his face with the back of a hand and let the boy get farther ahead. People spoke to him from the doorways in low, pleading tones. Brown faces wrinkled and cracked from age, weariness. Shopkeepers urged him inside. Once, as he crossed an alleyway, a young girl standing near a pile of empty boxes caught his eye and reached down to stroke her crotch invitingly.

At a beer counter, he stopped and drank and the heat leached the liquid immediately. Hurrying to catch up with his son, he stumbled into the back of an old woman who turned and hissed at him, a purely animal sound.

Philip apologized, tried straightening her mussed clothes, but finally rushed ahead to Mike and dragged him by the arm across the street to one of a dozen wrought iron tables in front of a small restaurant. The crowd surged around them. No one seemed to notice them and Philip felt invisible. All the beer had made him groggy and he realized after he'd sat that perhaps they should have turned back toward the hotel an hour ago. He really needed to lie down under the sharp chill of the air conditioner. For a moment he even wished for the cold weather back home.

"Hungry?"

Mike shrugged and searched the dark open doorway of the restaurant. From it curled the low pipes and high whining voice of a song on the radio.

"You think it's okay? Clean and all?"

"Why not? Let's sample the native delicacies, huh?" Philip's head buzzed and crackled. The smile felt heavy on his face. "Having a good time so far?" He immediately wanted to bite his tongue.

"Sure. A great time. Can't wait for the sailing though. It'll smell a lot better." The boy grinned and nodded.

The waiter came and brought with him a tattered menu on greasy thin paper. Mike ordered brusquely without looking up.

"What did you get?"

"A ham sandwich for you and some fried potatoes. And a beer."

Philip grimaced dramatically.

Mike stood sharply, clicking his shoes together. "I'll change it then. A Coke?"

Philip waved him down. "Just kidding. A beer's great. Hell, it won't matter much now anyway." He rubbed his oily face with the heels of his hands.

"Are you okay?" Mike asked.

"Yeah. Sure." Philip took a drink of the beer the waiter brought and noticed that Mike had ordered himself a tiny bottle of mineral water. He cleared his throat and sat forward, his elbows on the table. He looked directly into his son's eyes but the boy looked down and pried at the damp label on his drink.

"When I was in the Navy, after high school," Philip began, wondering what had made him think of this, "I sent a postcard home. . .you've seen it. . .the one of Wake Island from the air?"

Mike nodded and turned his chair toward the street.

"I wrote Mom. . .Grandmommie. . .that I'd already seen half the world. . .a cocky letter." He drank down the beer and motioned for another. "Anyway, what I really wanted to write was 'Come and get me. I made a mistake. Help.' It was awful," and he winced at the memory of himself standing alone on a street corner in his dress whites.

"Are you homesick there?" he blurted out. "Do you want to come home?" He hadn't meant to offer this solution. "I mean. . .you seem fine. . .all grown up all of a sudden. . .and all that other business about the dope. . ." Philip saw Mike's face turn rigid. "Mike, we didn't know what else to do, you know that. . .your mother was half crazy. . .me too. . .I. . ." His thoughts raced ahead and darted back to encompass all their troubles. And he knew he had to shut up, to stop talking. It was all old ground they'd paced bare already. But he was frightened, he realized, about his offer to take his son from the Academy. He couldn't quite understand where it had come from. He'd had no intention of saying it.

He was grateful when the waiter plunked down the fresh beer. Drinking it concentrated his headache between his eyes, but the silence helped settle his thoughts. Try not to fuck it up, he kept telling himself.

Mike turned and watched Philip drink. "It's great there. Really fine, no lie. I know you hated the Navy. That you were miserable there."

Philip almost reached out to touch the boy's arm.

"All that old stuff. . .those bad old days are gone. Really gone, Dad. I love the place. Honest."

The food came and Philip ate ravenously, hoping it might help clear his head. Mike hadn't ordered anything but a bottle of orange juice and the mineral water.

"Disgusting, isn't it?"

Philip turned, chewing, in the direction Mike nodded. Across the street a gaggle of children in stained shirts, few with pants, clustered around a couple of tourists and begged.

"Awful," Philip said.

"It really will be good to get out of all this. . . smells and trash on the streets and ugliness."

"Yeah."

"They could do better than this, you know." Mike set his jaw. "All that craziness at the airport, remember? And all this. . ." His arm swept a wide arc. "No sense of order. Of decency. Where's their leadership?"

Philip wanted to laugh and remind Mike of his own room a year ago but he looked up at the hard stare directed at the children and remained silent.

They finished and paid. Up the street Philip halted and put his hand on Mike's arm. "We should stop in one of those markets on the way back and buy your Mom a souvenir for Christmas. What do you say?"

"We could get a wall hanging, huh? A tapestry. She could see what they're supposed to look like."

Philip began defending Karen, but out of the corner of his eye he saw a horde of children cross the street and come toward them. Sweating again from the beer, he took the boy by the elbow and hurried uphill toward their hotel.

The next morning they took the short flight to the islands and instantly Philip was excited and relieved at leaving the squalor of the mainland behind. They moved back and forth across the narrow aisle of the ancient DC-3 to catch glimpses of the high green mountains fading into the rising gray mist from the ocean.

"You know," Mike pointed toward the receding range of foothills, "there're jaguars down there. David, one of my suite-mates, said so. His father comes down for a hunt. Now that'd be something to do, huh? Stalking something like that in thick jungle."

"Better than sailing?" Philip looked over the boy's shoulder and out the window.

"Of course not. . .just different."

The old plane rocked against the steady ocean breeze and soon they were over the water.

"The President's absolutely right, you know. Only two hours from us. We'll have to protect our national interests right here and farther south in Nicaragua. We may have to commit troops, too. No way around it." Mike nodded emphatically.

Philip listened quietly to his son's new politics pieced together from his military geopolitics lectures and he realized how much his own understanding of the area came to him diluted by the *Houston Post* and *Newsweek*. The boy's logic and arguments were compelling. He had a flood of statistics at hand.

"But some people think it'll be Vietnam again," Philip said. "That we don't belong in the middle of a country's civil unrest. That we only shore up what's already completely rotten and too far gone."

Mike shook his head and grinned. "Oh, Dad, that's just silly. And it's dangerous politics. The military knows what it has to do." The boy glanced back at the distant coastline. "If we'd held in Vietnam—declared war—we probably wouldn't be down there now with the jaguars."

Philip shrugged, but he recalled his relief at being assigned to the Mediterranean fleet instead of the Gulf of Tonkin. Some sailors had died in Saigon.

In twenty minutes the creaking plane rumbled to a stop at the far end of a rocky strip built out into the water. They had to walk back the entire length of the field to the rusting tin shack that served as a terminal. And while they were going through customs needlessly for the second time since they'd landed in the country, Philip saw Mike snap ramrod straight in his casual sailing clothes, his hands cupped along the seams of his white pants.

The small soldier across the low dirty table from them pried clumsily at Mike's Pentax until the lens finally popped off into his palm.

Mike reached over the luggage and touched the soldier's arm. He spoke in a low growl and the soldier glared at him and drew back, his hands still clutching the camera.

"What's wrong?" Philip asked, mopping his forehead with a damp handkerchief. Behind him the two other passengers muttered in Spanish.

"Stupid bastard's probably exposed my film. Maybe ruined the lens mount." Mike reached over the table for his camera. The soldier's eyes narrowed as his hand dropped to rest on his pistol scabbard.

Philip shook his head in disbelief. "Dammit, Mike! Just leave him alone."

But the boy ignored him and spoke quietly and evenly

to the young soldier who looked menacingly at him for a moment and then carelessly tossed the lens and camera into the open bag.

"What'd you say?" Philip asked. He felt the breaths of the Hondurans on his neck and sweat trickled down his stomach in the airless room.

Mike rearranged the camera in his nylon bag and zippered it shut with one fluid motion. "Asked to see his superior officer, that's all." Mike pulled his shoulder strap over his shoulder and turned his face close to Philip's. "Works better here than it would at Sheridan." The boy smiled. "These jerks probably aren't as good as the South Vietnamese Army."

As Mike plowed his way through the crowded shack, Philip cautiously pushed his bag toward the soldier and smiled sheepishly as he pried at a stuck latch.

In the rattling, cramped Chevy van on the way to the harbor, Mike seethed and mumbled as he cleaned his camera and remounted the lens. But Philip left him alone. Instead he took in scenery—the red road a complicated network of connecting potholes like the East Texas back roads of his childhood. Palms, the heavy pods of coconuts dangling obscenely from the undersides of their branches, lined the road. Looking up into the thick vegetation of the hills, he noticed a dozen shades of green from deep emerald to lime. When the bus descended the hills and the wide sweep of perfectly blue bay broke before them, Philip promised to give himself over to sailing and let go of all the tension. They'd have a fine time, he was positive, and they could talk for a week about navigation and sharks and whatever else the reefs offered them. And after a week of talking and sailing, he was certain that everything would be back to normal between them. They could be like they were years ago, long before the crazy days and the divorce.

They spent a busy morning at the marina. Mike asked to come with him to the chart briefing and Philip was proud of how good the questions were he asked the manager, who warned them of dangerous passages, private cays, and jagged coral reefs that lay invisible just below the surface.

At one point Mike corrected a bearing the old man offered and Philip laughed while the manager blushed and promised to name some deserted cay after the boy. Philip saw how pleased Mike was as he bowed his head over the charts.

By eleven they were out beyond the mouth of the harbor and well past the old upturned hull of a boat that marked some sailor's folly. They tacked constantly to accustom themselves to the boat.

Philip was amazed at the boy's agility and willingness to grapple with the tailing lines and winches. It was as if all the lessons he'd given him in the past—and which he'd paid little attention to at the time—had taken hold at last. At the wheel now, the wind over his left shoulder and the boat riding easily over the slight swells, Philip was happy. Happier than he could remember being in years. Maybe ever. The boat wasn't a bit sluggish but responded readily under his touch and the wind hummed in the rigging.

He caught glimpses of Mike coming and going below as he passed the hatchway. He'd volunteered to fix sandwiches for lunch and in turn Philip had agreed to an unscheduled stop at the mouth of a small bay for snorkeling before they pushed on across a narrow channel to their first anchorage at a deserted cay.

"You want cheese with it?" Mike asked, his face at the hatchway.

"Sure. Whatever you're having will be fine with me."

The sea here at a hundred feet was the deepest, richest blue Philip had ever seen. Relaxing his grip on the wheel, he stared down into it. The last time they'd been sailing together had been two years ago; he and Karen and Mike along with the Petersens. It was only a day sail on a nearby lake, but by noon his family had argued a dozen times. All the Petersens looked sorrowful. And finally Mike had holed up below, purposefully and methodically working his way through all the snacks on board. Philip's knuckles had been white on the wheel and that night his fingers cramped from the strain.

"Here," Mike handed him a sandwich wrapped in paper towel. "I'll take over now. You go ahead and eat."

"You first. I can wait."

"Go on. I've eaten." Mike took the wheel out from under Philip's hand.

Philip ate quickly and then went forward to stretch out on the deck. The sun was directly overhead, and despite the cool, constant breeze he could feel its heat.

He lay still for a long time and pictured the boy on the parade ground, or bent over his textbooks during the forced study period.

Finally he turned onto his stomach and, squinting from the glare, looked back at his son in the cockpit. The boy had his eye ahead on their destination. His face was strong and Philip felt admiration for his son grow in him quite unexpectedly. He wanted to slip back to the wheel and pull the boy to him, take his arms and rest Mike's head on his shoulder. But then he remembered the long white fingers stroking the oily metal of the soldier's gun and the look of disgust in Mike's eyes as the children had crowded the tourists. And he lay back on the deck and watched the water glide past.

Other images came and went, drifted past his closed eyelids as gently as the water flowed under the bow. The boat pitched and rolled more as Mike altered their course a little, but by this time Philip was asleep.

Philip had let Mike snorkel over the reefs for two hours and now he was afraid the sudden tropical night would catch them outside their anchorage. He pushed the throttle forward and heard the boat's diesel drum rapidly.

They had just taken the sails down and Mike stood on the bow. The deserted cay, flat and lush with palms and mangroves, lay to their right only a hundred yards away. Philip knew that in order to reach their small bay he had to round a promontory and head straight in, due south. But he was uncertain about how far he should lay off the point of land.

The fathometer mounted on the cockpit wall in front of him raced through numbers as the bottom below them bristled with coral and rising sandbars and sank abruptly into deep troughs. Ten feet. Eight. Twenty-one. Nine.

"Do you see anything?" Philip cupped his hand and yelled forward. He watched Mike shield his eyes from the sun as he peered into the water.

"It's hard to tell. Angle of light's screwing things up."

Philip nodded, glanced down at the open charts and aerial photographs on the bench beside him and then looked quickly at the red numbers on the fathometer. Ten. Six. Fifteen.

The sun was just above the horizon and Philip knew how suddenly night came on down here. Perhaps he should anchor now, he thought. But he didn't want to spend the night unprotected. He had been silly to let Mike swim for so long. But watching him, after his own brief swim, was pure delight. The boy swam energetically as if he could take everything in at once. "You wouldn't believe what's down here," he yelled. And every time he'd surfaced for a quick breath of air he'd shouted out some new discovery.

Then the fathometer went black and the boat lurched once and shuddered her entire length. Underneath them the fiberglass moaned at the contact. Then the boat was free for a second before the keel rammed into a solid wall of coral and jerked to a halt.

Quickly Philip reached for the throttle and at the same instant looked forward for Mike. But he wasn't there.

"Mike!" Philip slipped the engine into neutral. The boat caught the swells broadside and rocked sharply, its keel locked in a coral vise.

"Mikey!" Philip stepped up from the cockpit and ran the few feet to the bow.

Mike lay sprawled on the deck, his hand on his forehead.

"Are you alright?" Philip knelt and gently removed the boy's hand. His breath caught at the sight of blood from a long shallow gash on his forehead.

Mike sat up and shook his head. Then he stood unsteadily as Philip clutched him, his arm around the boy's waist.

"I'm fine." Mike wiped the bloody hand on his swim trunks. "It's not deep. See, it's already stopped bleeding. Damned line caught me. I should have been braced better. My fault."

"Come on." Philip pulled Mike back to the cockpit and threw open the locker under the bench seats. He pawed out a life jacket and stood fumbling with the straps and buckles.

"Dad, I'm fine. See."

"Here, get into this."

The boy mopped at his forehead and pushed the jacket away. "What are you doing? It's just a nick."

Philip stepped close to the boy and brusquely stuffed his arm into the bulky jacket. Then, manhandling him, he turned Mike around and began adjusting the buckles. His hands fumbled with the metal fasteners.

Mike was dazed for a moment. Then, stepping back, he shook his head vehemently. "What are you *doing*? I'm a good swimmer, you know that."

"We've got to get off. Get to shore," Philip shouted up at him as he sat to pull on his shoes.

"This is crazy. You can't leave the boat sitting out here. Come on, let's try reverse." Mike sat behind the wheel and reached for the throttle but Philip caught his hand in midair and pulled him up and shoved him toward the stern.

"Shit." Mike pushed his father away, kicked at him with his tennis shoes. But Philip kept shoving the boy.

"Listen, we've only run aground a little. We're not sinking, for God's sake. You've showed me how to take care of this a hundred times. Come on, let me try. Let's sit down and talk this over."

"Too late to talk," Philip yelled. All he could hear was the coral scraping the hull. He imagined Karen sitting on her couch, her hands cupped in her lap, her eyes locked on him, awaiting an explanation.

"Dammit, listen to me. You can't leave the boat. You're in charge. The captain. It's your responsibility. At the Academy they say. . ."

"Goddamn the goddamned Academy. *You're* my responsibility. Not this fucking boat." And though Mike still talked, the grating keel filled Philip's ears.

Finally he pushed Mike over the side and jumped after him, grabbing a handful of orange life jacket.

Mike flailed. "Let go of me, dammit. You'll drown both of us. Let go."

But Philip swam with swift strong strokes, towing the boy behind him.

In a few minutes they felt the coral under their shoes and stood in chest-deep water. Mike dumbly followed his father now as they carefully picked their way over the sharp coral. Philip could feel it underfoot lacerating his shoes. Twice Mike stumbled but Philip caught him and with his arms around the boy's shoulders he guided him onto the narrow strip of beach.

Philip sat heavily and yanked Mike down by his side. He closed his eyes and lay back on the warm sand. Pelicans squawked and dove for food nearby. Over that and the noise of the surf the diesel engine pounded away steadily.

Mike stood and stripped off the vest. "My God, you didn't even shut off the engine."

Philip sat up and rubbed his face. He looked out at the silhouette of the boat rocking with the swells. "Mike, I want you to come home. Forget Sheridan. Everything'll be fine. It'll be okay now."

"No." Mike shook his head, walked back out into the water and began picking his way through the coral.

Philip stood and walked after him. "Michael!"

Mike faced him, the low golden light of the sun striking his face. His close-cropped hair glistened. "I think I can get it off the bottom before dark. Somebody has to."

After a moment Philip turned away from the look in the boy's eyes. Then he walked farther down the beach and sat watching the pelicans dive along the sprawling reef. They had six more days of sailing left.

THE asphalt road turns twice to the north-northwest — once before the bridge that cuts the blood-red creek ineffectually with its shadow and once again, six-tenths of a mile further on. Like the curls on a baby's head. Two really. Both in the northerly direction. And the pines, perennially, come down to the very edge of the asphalt to look at who or what passes.

Usually they look down on my people because almost all of my relatives live somewhere along a stretch of that main road or up dirt side roads that are deserts in the summer and impassable bogs with the winter rains. Uncle John came running down such a road that late August night; no full moon, no shoes, the white floury sand pulled up by his old toes and still falling after the sounds of his chest and legs and arms had passed on. The sand puddling behind him, mounding up in a certain distinctive way so that if Dewitt Williamson, the old justice of the peace, had seen the prints, he could have figured out whose they were. Hand in his pocket fingering his knife and by extension his right testicle. "Nigra. Nigra or a slightly built woman." Just like I'd heard him say once before and I'd looked at the others and he'd fingered and we'd all looked away into the summer-green pine tops and beyond the buzzard floating high, worried by three loud crows. And we'd all smiled.

"You can tell with the shoes on?"

"Shore." The ball-knife slowed. "Shore I can." As if to add, You can't? You really can't?

The noise of the falling sand. A mysterious soft sound down close to the uneven surface of the road. Obliterated to the runner by the Porters' two goddamn bulldogs that are great for raising hell but do it discreetly from underneath either the body of the '56 two-tone blue Chevy with a sticker on the shattered rear window that reads "Built in Texas by Texans," or from underneath the askew front porch, where the more cowardly of the two, Backbone, always hides.

He passed his first wife's closed house in the bend before the road straightened and ran over a creek full of car bumpers and hubcaps and stoves with porcelain pocked by twenty-twos and birdshot. "Goddamn dogs," he yelled over his shoulder. Not sparing a single thought for long dead Beverly whose house remained locked behind him and still except for the six-foot chicken snake that moved openly, even in daylight, even on bone-cold days, from furnitured room to stocked kitchen shelves. As youngsters we'd all seen it through the dirty windows.

And flying over the wooden bridge, for a second, he was proud that not a single rusted hubcap belonged to him or would have belonged to his son if he'd been fortunate enough to have one. Then onto the asphalt, a pivot of the foot that tore the skin, puckered and stretched it and forced it away from the flesh.

He could still hear the deep snore. Still see the slack mouth that hung open in the darkened room across the bridge and around the bend at his back. Still. And he shuddered, feeling certain that her mouth was slowly closing, inch by inch, with every dry suck of his chest. He ran along the center stripe because the pine trees, which came down to the very edges of the road, had cracked and buckled the soft asphalt with their roots.

I know what the little circle on my calendar tells me. Half-moon. Moon on the wane. The half-closed eye of it giving the ripe Spanish mulberries, deep purple by day, a black cast. Giving him enough light to follow the dull yellow stripe. The skin of the one foot ripped through now and flapping like a shoe in need of a half-sole. A car with a flat tire.

Not having been gassed in the First World War enabled him to run the three miles. He'd lied and told the nice but deadly serious man that he was eighteen. And he wasn't gassed because he'd learned from someone older—seventeen—that you didn't stay in the shallow places. Despite the clatter of machine guns, you scrambled out of the trench or shell crater, came rolling out and tried to wedge something or someone between you and the German guns. And let the yellow gas pass away. When it went from yellow to white it was a sure sign.

And he'd never smoked, unlike his youngest brother, my father, who smoked more than anyone I've ever known. Also, Uncle had a horseshoe above his door when he was young, a little boy. And so do I, across the room over the door that opens onto the kitchen from the hallway. And I don't smoke at all. Like my mother's people. And I inherited a bulbous nose from her, a secret loathing for light-skinned and light-haired people and a hint, diluted in me, of Baptist morality.

And when he was there, at Mrs. Cumming's door, when he'd arrived, he was still able—although nearly naked from the waist up and almost frothing like a hard-run horse, the white hairs on his chest and back plastered down flat—to stick his fist through the single plate glass panel of the aluminum door.

Standing there, he closed his eyes for the first time since he'd heard her on the couch. Ever since he'd waked to piss, had lain on his side debating the coldness of the tiles against the expanding throb of his bladder, he hadn't even blinked. He was afraid of pulling his hand back out, still thanking God there hadn't been a wooden door behind this glass one.

The dogs inside came viciously to life. Toenails ripping across the wooden floor. Mrs. Cummings too hardened—so old that no one remembered there having been a Mr. Cummings—to act shy in the least.

"What the hell?" She slept naked on the screen porch. The opened bamboo blinds and the moon playing a tune on her wrinkled skin that for Uncle was neither frightening nor cacophonous.

"It's me. Me!" Her only neighbor for miles whom she knew by the shape of his body as it moved against the treeline two hundred yards away or by the sound of the loud snort he used to clear his head—never spitting or swallowing but just making a dry sound—the sound she'd heard him make out of sight when she'd visited Edith. The fist through her door only mildly upset her. There were good reasons for almost everything imaginable. It seemed he'd bent the soft aluminum scrollwork that decorated the door.

"What'll I do?" he moaned. "I know she's dead."

Her flanks glowed and blurred as she pushed his fist back through and unlatched the single drop hook that kept him out. She shushed the little dog at her feet and, with the door opened, he noticed that her toenails were painted, dark in the deep shadow of the porch.

"Sit down here and wait." She moved off, the toenail sounds of the dogs following. From the dark came an old thin shirt and a glass of water. She remained above him in the reduced light, robeless. "What's the matter?"

"What'll I do with Belle now? What'll I do with Belle?"

I've been on that porch. Not at night and not under similar circumstances. But I know he must have felt a bit comforted after the run from the motionless, deeply snoring wife on the couch where she slept to avoid waking him—although he'd been retired for five years and only woke up early to fish or hunt and trap depending on the season. Mrs. Cummings took the glass and went back inside to phone—something Uncle hadn't thought of once since he'd reached down to touch her cheek.

But nothing would have saved her, their doctor said, and the next Friday, the unusually chilly morning of the funeral, Mother drove. Quietly dressed in shades of gray, she was a miniature behind the huge steering wheel. Up on the crocheted pillows and hunched over, she looked like a child. Like I must have looked years ago when she'd taught me to drive on these same narrow country roads. Years before my father'd died. His heart had virtually exploded, the general practitioner said. Massive and complete. He had keeled over in the guard shack he'd retired to. His little red-and-white–striped pole down across the plant entrance, the weighing scale blocked. "Hey, wake up. Shit! Wake up." The driver, red-eyed, tired and hyper from the bennies, pecking on the glass with the metal butt of his closed pocket knife.

And because he's dead and my mother's innocuous, we come and go among all our relatives' houses. Between John and Edith's and the other brothers'. They all hope we spread the tales and gossip and rumors because none of them have spoken to one another in years. But I don't, even when Mother calls me up to "pump" me for the "gossip," as she calls it.

The woods closed in, the tops of the trees meeting over the road. I felt hot even with my window halfway down. "What'll he do now?"

She would never turn her eyes from the road, not even for an instant. "Put her away maybe. Keep her. Nobody'll like it. No matter what he does."

Belle. The only woman I'd ever known named that. Their retarded daughter, physically grown at forty-five and stronger than most men at that age. The morning of Edith's death she'd played a game with herself. Every time someone called to express their sorrow and to say they were bringing over casseroles, she'd answered and said what she always said, ever since I can remember her, "Hello to hello." Then she'd chuckle and slam down the receiver. The joke, her joke, somehow pulled to her satisfaction. John, lying on his bed, too tired to come in and wrestle with her. To talk quietly to her while she wailed softly like a calf. And Edith was dead and so couldn't pinch her flabby, milk-white arms until, the flesh mottled and bruising, she'd stop, lurch out of her mother's grip and stand looking at the floor. Finally, my mother'd shaken her shoulders hard, rattled her teeth and she'd stopped without a single sound.

"He's pretty lost without Edith."

How many times had we said her name lately? Even my mother, who fought such a hard and constantly disappointing struggle to consider herself a Christian, even she despised her. They all did for reasons that may have been perfectly good ones years ago, but since had become something almost mythic and, like myth, rootless now, free-floating. Able to absorb the stray pieces of gossip. Accumulate to itself stories and random tales in which she, Edith, always stood waiting, at the center of the labyrinth. Just patiently waiting for all their ill fortune. Behind her was John, whom she'd taken away from them all. The mother, brothers, and their wives.

A cardinal. Two. Flew from their roosts and swooped down low in front of the car. And a dog, limping on its hind legs, came up viciously at us from the bar ditch. The woods were thick at our sides. Twilight and still like it was almost dark instead of mid-morning.

You see, the land between Patroon and Norman isn't at all like the land just this side of the Laotian border. Where this is rolling hills, there the land must have once blossomed upwards toward the sky and, having hung on too long, cascaded earthward in a tangle of boulders and trees. Someone said that it was just plain eerie countryside and I guess that's true. Both there and here are covered with trees and undergrowth. But here, alone or with someone else within hailing distance, both of you quiet and motionless on a deer-stand, when the small whitetail buck flicks its tail and jerks up its head to sort out your movement as too sudden and unnatural from the other movements and looks you in the eye the second before you squeeze the trigger—the look whiteless because the eye is a solid brown or black—that one look, that exchange—you, through the enclosed, limited world in the scope, and him, judging the dead ground in between and his next springing move—is natural, instinctive on his part.

There, the eye is brown or black too, but with too much white showing because of the fear. And there's no instinct, but the moment before you squeeze off the round you see on the face the painful desire to be that animal, or any animal that can push aside the foliage visually and hope to see what's crucial and then to move quickly before a finger comes slowly all the way back. But it can't and you, in the same situation, can't either. And when you're on the other end, crouched in what you think is a place charmed against steel-jacketed bullets, you feel those unnatural, uninstinctive eyes looking at you from motionless places where only snakes and the enemy would hide. And always you're frightened, no matter which end you're on.

So, it was John who, because my father, his brother, has been dead for a long time, tried to take me back into the woods the first fall, the first week of deer season I was back home for good. And he failed. I walked back down the old logging road to the pickup and drank down the coffee oblivious to its cold, bile bitterness.

"You alright?" He stood by the opened door ejecting the shells onto the cracked vinyl seat. I nodded over the steamless cold metal cup of the thermos. He stood looking hard at me, but I stared straight ahead, more afraid, at that moment, of conversation than of anything else.

I saw him out of the corner of my eye. A smaller replica of my father. The hair the same, the eyes, the hoarse voice. Hoarse from chronic sinus trouble that lately I've noticed in myself. All the same, but in him honed down to a sharper, clearer relief. Smaller, dainty almost, but I'd never say that to him or to anyone. His smallness like the nervous quickness of a squirrel—alert and intolerant of sudden moves. Of sudden shifts of the body or of the subtle shifts in a voice.

He slid the gun into its case and zipped up the long, wrap-around zipper. Slid onto the seat and slammed the door.

"You're alright." And this time it wasn't a question. But I felt silly and unable to help myself at the moment or even to help his embarrassment. Unwilling to tear myself loose from the cup or the windshield and the narrow woods road before me.

"Let me tell you why your father never liked to hunt." Or dance. Or drink. Sometimes even laugh. I smiled and relaxed my grip on the smooth cup. It was our game. He'd started it a long time ago; I can't remember when, maybe on one of those afternoons when my mother still cried bent in a gentle curve over her sewing machine. Where she first sewed on all of his loose buttons and then hemmed all of his ragged cuffs so she could take the clothes down to the black church to give away. "Thank you, Sister Courtney," the grizzle-headed old man had said, patting me absentmindedly on the head. Or maybe it was later than that. Anyway, it began with the truth—my mother said that—and each time after, he'd altered it, made it funnier. Had taken away, slowly, the terror and humiliation that lingered a bit at the back of it all.

"You remember it was Apollo Morgan, don't you?" He leaned forward to start the engine. I nodded and he'd go on about how Daddy'd scotched the Assembly of God preacher's plans to walk on water with the aid of a pine scaffold just below the river's muddy, swirling surface.

"Took the boards out, far out in the middle. The old man almost drowned." And he'd begin to fabricate. Pass quickly over the long, swift strokes of his papa who'd swum before the whole crowd to my daddy, bent double with laughter on the opposite bank, and in front of half the county—half there to scoff and half to believe—had whipped him with his fists.

He'd passed over it that day. Dwelled, instead, on the people on the bank. Trying to get me to remember people who'd died fifteen years before I was born. "Your cousin Bobby was there." He reached over and took the cup from my hands and slung the coffee out the window. "We'll make some fresh when we get home."

Not everyone attended the funeral. Only a few friends and Mother and me and John. And his two brothers, J. L. and Tom. But not their wives. All of us on the uncomfortable folding chairs. The silence before it all got started interrupted by suppressed coughs, choked off quickly, and by the shuffling of feet on the scarred linoleum. By words spoken in harsh undertones to squirming children.

At the front of the small frame church, Edith was laid out in the too sensuously plush lining of the coffin, looking strangely beautiful and twenty years, three heart attacks, younger. Beautiful and firm-jawed and young. As young as they all had been before they'd started hating one another. The family in old photographs—the men looking sheepish, their hair shiny and flat against their heads, and the women skinny in rolled-up trousers with dangling cigarettes in their mouths and hair smooth on top, falling suddenly into huge, fuzzy curls. Of all of us on the front row, only John had continued to admire her, to live under her sway. And me too, in a way, because her hardness and selfishness were almost virtues because they never wavered.

Out of the corner of my eye, and leaning forward a bit, I could see them all in profile. John, next to me, his face contorted. The swollen foot in a moccasin split from the toe upwards, wrapped tightly, the elastic bandage stretched. Then Belle, her face blank and tear-stained because the others were crying. Like him, in a way, nervous and calm at the same time. Then Mother and J. L.

J. L. must look like someone I've never seen, like some relative everyone's forgotten. He doesn't look like Daddy or John or Tom. Big, garrulous, suffering constantly from a bleeding ulcer, he drinks half-and-half from a quart carton and munches pieces of melba toast he's carefully lined up on a windowsill that morning, next to his reclining chair. Watching him made me think of Ruth, his wife, who never could completely get the grit out of her cooking so that spoons scrape across the bottoms of bowls of peas. "I'm real sorry," she'd say. "Didn't wash 'em enough, I guess." And raise her already arched eyebrows ceilingwards.

That day, with the weak-lunged organ playing, I could picture what had gone on earlier. The yellow early morning sunlight ineffectually checked by the partially closed blinds. The matriarch, the mother of the four men, endlessly rocking, her braided hair falling down the side of the rocker and onto the floor.

"You'd better go on if you're goin'. "

"What?"

"You heard me."

The old woman's heavy breasts, almost too monstrous to heave with her shallow breaths, fell to where her black plastic belt crossed her swollen stomach. She nodded as if she'd heard too.

"Can't believe she's dead." But J. L.'s voice was calm, unconcerned. He skillfully broke a flat piece of toast into equal parts.

Ruth shook her head at him as he tipped the carton of cream. "You goin'?"

J. L. nodded and looked across at the old deaf woman

fingering her hair, rocking gently over the scarred oak planks of the floor. "What'll he do now?"

"And there's the girl."

"She even laid out his underwear at night."

The old woman shivered, unaware of the other two people, and pulled her gaudy afghan closer around her shoulders.

"She whistled and he jumped."

"And the girl too." He tipped back the carton.

"It's a thousand wonders she didn't figure out some way to take him with her."

—*Standing on the promises that shall not fail*—

We all stood—the women sang loudly and off-key; the men didn't try at all or just mouthed the words. At the far end of the row Tom stood against the glare of the frosted glass. The translucent swirls of white muddied with streaks of brown and dark red. Tom was dark against the snow-glare of the light—silhouetted in his crisp khaki pants and shirt that he starched and ironed himself. Still able to find clothes that weren't permapressed. His old-fashioned ankle-high boots clean and brightly shined. Against this light like he must have been this morning against the early sun. Awakened in the dark early hours by the ring of his wife's bell. Nevada, whom we all call Vada, calling to be drugged again against the sharp pains along her spine.

He'd drug her there—in the darkened room lighted only by a cool blue night-light like the one you'd buy for an infant's nursery. And later, when the day nurse showed up around seven, he'd go out to putter amongst his pieces of statuary. His acre of solid shapes. Tom slowly moving, straightening here and there, brushing away the highway dust, leveling a fountain on the gravel. Down amongst the ceramic birdbaths and painted Negro midgets with fishing pole in hand or arm out expressing a contented desire to hold some horse's reins. The arthritis causing him to clamp his lips in a firm, straight line echoed by the crude features of the nymphs and angels whose own lifelessness and stiffness had always been tied, in my mind, to their own minute raised lines that ran down their foreheads and noses and bisected their own clenched, toothless mouths. That line ran through everything on his cluttered acre — through the bunches of grapes and entwined snakes of bas-reliefs on the sides of fountains and through the ugly urns for plants like mother-in-law tongue and wandering Jew. The line created by the molding process when the cumbersome molds are joined and wet slip funneled in.

The phone'd ring but he wouldn't hear. "It's one of the most pop'lar." He'd stand back and turn the gritty piece of cheap pottery for the morning's first customer, who'd stopped because the two of them shared a similar love of art.

"I'll take a couple. Can you pack 'em in a box?"

He'd nod and clamp his teeth together again.

I wondered that morning what all of those things had said to him. It was Tom who got Edith interested in his art of pouring clay into metal molds. Years ago they'd talked for one whole Saturday afternoon in the backyard at Edith's, under the wooden grape arbor. I was little and I'd watched them from behind a hedge. At first it was a game but suddenly I realized that I'd need to sneak away and not, as I'd planned, burst out on them.

And later, that same day, both of them laughing and smiling, she'd asked John to build her a shop behind the house where she too could practice, to her own satisfaction, on urns and fountains and little Negroes.

That interminable afternoon of the funeral. The day almost entirely taken up with short trips. From my house to Mother's and then to church. From there to the grave. And then home again to change and then on to John's. Most of the afternoon I'd tried to get to him through the line of mourners who passed by the couch where he sat in his rumpled suit—

pale and quiet. But I couldn't and only once he'd looked across at me, my tea glass raised, the condensed water dripping onto my shirt front. He'd raised his clenched hand from the arm of the couch but only a fraction and then dropped it back again. His gaze slid away from mine and out the sliding glass doors down to Edith's shop.

The crowds thinned and thickened. People came and went. Casseroles littered the big round oak table. Belle, untended, content, went from group to group to listen for some mention of her mother. I watched friends and neighbors and a couple of distant relatives form groups in the yard. Starting and stopping like erratic bees moving from bush to bush. Stopped they looked like Tom's acre. Only the day itself showing any movement.

Finally, most of them left. John slept deeply in his bedroom. Belle, tired of her game, slept too, in the unnatural light of her pink room. Mother sat across the wrought iron table from me. The cement porch was cold to my bare feet.

"But why'd she do that?"

"Afraid of Lewis, her first husband. That he'd come back to her after he got out."

"So there wasn't any loot? He never got out of the bank."

Mother shook her head. Opened her mouth to answer but didn't. The clouds were too high to be serious, not even thick enough to block the low, feeble sun. Its light making our hands and our hot coffee reddish and golden in turns.

"She drove?"

"She drove off, they say. That's why she never drove again. Why she'd sweat at traffic lights even when she was just a passenger. Hated to listen to the engine idle." She sipped her coffee. Her jaw sagged, the flesh of her cheeks flabby. "It's the last time anyone trusted her."

"If it's all true."

"If it's all true. But she really did keep a gun under her

pillow. When they first married I use to come over and spend the night when your daddy and John were gone. And that first night she took it out of the chest of drawers and slid it up under the pillow. 'Two women all alone,' she said. But there was the story going round. And Lewis certainly was in the state pen."

"And you liked her back then?"

Mother still dressed in her somber colors, unnatural, almost an insult to the ripe August afternoon before us in the green of the yard and thick woods beyond the chain link fence. She smiled. "She was the most exciting thing in my life then. The newest and last sister-in-law. All of us outsiders together. All of us having to deal with Mama Courtney."

I looked across at her, her head turned to the yard, shaking gently on its own. The old photographs—not a colored one amongst them—my mother, all of them, at this place and that. The men in leather jackets which John had told me cost next to nothing.

"But soon there was trouble."

She nodded slowly. "She just wanted him alone, to herself. That's really not that bad. And then there was Belle and for a while they did move off. It seemed just far enough to keep us away. And when they did come back, Belle was twelve. She was ashamed of her, of course. Then it was harder. You kept them at home. They usually didn't live that long. Who knows what having that girl caused.

"Then when Mama had her stroke we all parted company. No one could agree on anything anymore. I guess everyone looked pretty mean-spirited, selfish, ugly. Though Edith took the cake in several ways. But who can remember half of it all, it's been so many years?"

"So J. L. ended up with her."

"He didn't have to. No one forced him." She snapped out and suddenly subsided. "You really ought to talk with him. Find out what he's going to do."

"I know."

"Come help me with the last of the dishes."

The sound woke me late that night. At first I thought I was back in that tired, semi-alert state I'd finally acquired over there after only a week and which lasted throughout the tour.

I had my clothes on but not my boots and my clammy cold feet told me I wasn't there but here among the trees and my family. I wasn't at the war despite the sound. Crump and crump. Deep and far away. At most a feeling that belongs entirely to the bones and not the ears. Felt in the bones and reverberating outward to the brain, slowly, by way of the blood. This sound the same as that other piece of warnoise. The high-altitude bombing from the B-52s that flew almost nightly forever to just beyond our horizon and deposited, as far as any of us could ever tell, only that dull bonenoise and nothing more. That noise that came, all the way from Guam, to vibrate within us, a singular serenade.

I lay on the couch that Edith had lain on. My head where hers had been. I felt both of us together in the dark. All the house quiet except for the noise.

But the sound wasn't rhythmical but sporadic. No set cadence conducive to sleep. I rolled back the covers, wadded them at my feet on the too short couch that had caused a sharp ache in the small of my back, and crossed the soft carpet. The noise was coming from Edith's "workshop," as she called it. Through the big sliding doors I could follow the downward slope of the backyard. A hundred or so feet down, partly obscured by some big fig bushes and a hedge, stood her house, full of the plaques and statuary she had produced in quantities over the last fifteen years. And just beyond the small frame house, the arbor where I'd seen Tom and her long ago swinging in the Renoir light.

The lights down there were on and through the single

window high up the side of the wall I could see a dim shadow pass in front of the light. The crump continued. The shadow moved and a fine dust-like flour eddied and swirled with the dark shape.

Nothing but that noise and the absolute quiet of the house, not a clock ticking anywhere to interfere with the violence just down the slight hill. I could see the fig bushes swaying in the wind but even that noise didn't penetrate.

"She's looking for the money." Mother had been standing by the cold fireplace all the time. She was in her robe, a glass of milk pale, almost iridescent, in her hand. She took a slow drink.

"I thought he never got to the car?"

She was silent for a moment. "Not that money. She told me that she hid some somewhere. Put away a little at a time from John's paycheck. She told everyone at one time or another. Almost everybody thought it was a joke."

"Why'd she do it?"

" 'Getting-away money,' she called it. For emergencies." Mother, small in the dark, her voice light and airy. "My stomach aches. Maybe the milk'll help."

I watched the shape down there move erratically before the pale light. The dust moving like it was alive. "She's wrecking the place."

Mother nodded. "Maybe you'd better go down and stop her. She might hurt herself."

I sat and pulled on my heavy boots, all the time watching the light in the small house.

"They're all coming tomorrow."

"What?"

"J. L., Tom. Everyone. For the afternoon."

"Why?"

"John suggested I ask them. And they all wanted to."

"I'll go down and clean up the mess."

"Tom'd be hurt if he saw it."

The crump would stop for a moment then continue with added frenzy. Despite the closeness of the room I shivered. The heat had been turned off for the summer and the small, decorative fire had burned down right after our quiet supper. Mother turned and left while I patted down the old soft family quilts wishing I could crawl back under them and cover my head and sleep until they all came and relieved the tension or made it worse—did something.

When I slid the heavy glass door open, the wind seemed to quicken and the noise had come up to the house so audibly because it blew from the south, up around the small workshop and against the house. The smaller limbs of the live oaks creaked and the heavier ones—as thick as a man's thigh— groaned lowly. But there was no hint of the coolness of this morning. Instead, from the south—the Gulf a hundred miles away—this wind was humid and warm. Palpable.

I gathered up my baggy pajama bottoms. Bent down and folded them into the tops of my boots.

Around the other side, away from the house, the wooden door was open and the wind had thrown back the light aluminum screen, had jammed it under the sloping supports of the wooden porch.

John, in an old robe pulled tightly around him, stood up on the porch just out of the light.

"Belle?"

He turned and waved me away. His eyes showed too much white. His body shook under the terrycloth.

"Is it Belle?"

He motioned vaguely toward the light and over his shoulder I watched her walk in the thick dust. Like a wraith. Her naked body something I hadn't seen since we were children.

The flesh shiny white from the dust. The breasts small and sagging as if they'd melted and run down her chest. The nipples golden in the light and erect. Her stomach tight and the muscles of her thighs and back like those of a gymnast. All of this always before covered by a shapeless dress like a tent.

"Stop her."

He shook his head. Turned, his teeth showing between his lips. "No."

She moved at random with the claw hammer held out before her as if it threatened her. Parts of the wall plaques she'd smashed still swung slowly on their wire hangers. Gaudily colored prayers and homilies about the hearth and God and home.

She moved back and forth and the wind sucked some of the dust away from her and out around us to the open air. She never looked our way but kept on with her work. Broke the plaques and then the fountains and birdbaths. The heavy gritty urns, the crouched lions with flowerpots in their backs. Then she'd squat and dig through the pieces with the handle of the hammer.

"I'll stop her." But his hard hand stopped me, pushed at my chest. He grabbed my arm and turned us away.

"She's looking for money, you know. Her mother always told her it was for leaving." He wasn't talking to me directly but to the night, the warm, moist wind, the clashing leaves of the head-high fig bushes.

"She guessed what I've been thinking. You see? 'Gettin'-away money.' That's what her mother said it was for."

"I see. Listen . . ." But he wasn't hearing. On the horizon the light from the airport fifteen miles away flashed. Then was gone. Then flashed again.

"That night in the hospital they wanted to take off her false eyelashes. The nurse bent down low over the bed, but I stopped her. 'Leave her alone,' I said. She never let anyone see her without her makeup on."

"So leave her alone." He jerked his thumb over his shoulder. "She'll get tired after awhile." He pulled his bathrobe tight and stepped down off the porch. I gave him enough time to get inside the house before I followed.

Mother saw us off after breakfast.

"You know how to get there?" John asked. And she nodded. Belle had gone back to bed and none of us mentioned the night before.

The day of Edith's funeral had been unseasonably cool, but the contrast of it to the heat before and after—the stifling humidity of early August—made it seem as if a cold front, a blue norther, had swept down from the Panhandle. It's football weather, that's what my father would have said. And Mother described it, when I drove over to her house the morning of the funeral, as mint in the air.

But now there wasn't the slightest hint of fall. No wind like the night before. The road through the pines to the river bottom a crooked line of ankle-deep white dust. Both of us sweating at nine in the morning, the windows shut against the boiling dust, the vents closed, the temperature at least 120 where the sun angled in low, unimpeded by a single cloud, and struck the blue metal and vinyl of the dashboard. The dust fine enough to get through the vent doors and swirl gently down around our legs.

I wanted to mention last night. Belle. The whole thing, but he looked straight ahead and down the road. And soon we were in the bottom. The woods tight around us. The sudden movements of small, invisible birds grating on my nerves. You could feel the rear tires slip in the deep sand banked up at the curves.

"Finally got an electrician. Couldn't get around to doing it myself." I remembered that two summers ago we'd gone down to the camp house on the river that he'd built all by himself.

We'd just poked around and he'd talked. Usually just like father. Unable to really build anything properly. Tables wobbled, sawed corners refused to meet squarely, tools ran off and hid. But he'd been successful on this camp house, stood beside it proudly. And even then I hadn't known what to say. Just smiled and nodded. Followed him around and patted what he patted.

Down in the green light, cool as if the heat had been subtly filtered away by the millions of pine needles over our heads, the black fresh tar paper that covered the sides was a shock that didn't diminish.

We'd spent the afternoon together, not mentioning the place I was headed for in a few weeks. He drank a Coke as I drank a Schlitz I'd brought from town. One of his old black-and-tans rubbing up against us, then hunkering down for a stroke.

Now on our drive down, the trees began to sway as the hot August wind rose. The dearest memory of my father, I recalled, wasn't one from my youth nor one from just before his death, but a memory from the dead ground of my middle teens when nothing seems to have stood out and nothing now seems to remain except that afternoon, hot like the sweltering ride in this pickup. The canebrake rattlesnake he'd killed tied in diagonally across the rusted-out pickup bed. Eight feet long and over.

And he'd said, "Here, don't be afraid. It can't hurt you now, don't you know that?" And I'd stroked the flat triangular head numb with fear, almost laid out by it. Numb and as glassy-eyed as the cat's eyes in that snake's head. Afraid then and then afraid later over there and even now because of the trees and darkness of the woods and because I had nothing to say to someone else afraid too. Because she was dead and his real child couldn't understand. And I wasn't fit to help.

Once there, we opened the windows in silence and propped open the door to air out the inside. And we sat on the porch in metal chairs gummy from a dozen paintings.

Finally, everyone came. J. L.'s car bottoming out in the holes. The uncomfortable scraping of muffler and gas tank reached us before the sound of the engine. His Cadillacs are always a year or two wrong. The fins always a bit too large. And behind the tires the metal is always peppered with flecks of rust and tiny holes as if it'd been shot from close range with bird shot.

J. L. and Tom talked endlessly about nothing. Their voices unfailing and soporific in the afternoon heat. John dozing, his chair leaned back against the rough planking of the house front. Ruth and Mother inside fixing sandwiches.

In the heat, wasps flew lethargically. Vada stayed in the car, while Mama Courtney charged through the briars with her walker. Fuzzed up her short hose, and stood against the dazzling light, looking down into the river.

"Mama? Mama's gone." Vada would call from the hot, ticking car. The oil still dripping through the engine.

After awhile, after the sandwiches had been eaten and the sun was setting, Mother suggested a campfire on the sand-bar downstream, east of the house. But we couldn't find Belle until Tom, his khakis wilted from the heat, limp and baggy, called out that she was up under the house lying in the flat-bottom boat.

"Goddammit Belle, come out from under there." John suddenly embarrassed by Belle, who'd been that way for forty-five years.

"Come on, honey." Mother cooing. All of us bent over. The three dogs, tied to the separate corners of the house, bored with the whole thing.

"I can't see you. You can't hear me." Her eyes clenched shut, her hands neatly crossed on her chest. "No more hello to hello."

John turned and went around to the wooden steps. Bent

down we could see his legs beyond Belle and farther, beyond him, the opened car doors and Vada idly fanning herself with a road map.

We dragged the boat out with Belle laughing at the sudden smooth ride across the pine needles, unable to keep her eyes shut. She sat up. "Hello to hello again." She wanted a longer ride in the boat.

We all walked in the dark down to the river. The path white under the deep blue sky, the stars just beginning to show. The woods and the river cooling off, emanating a dampness and fustiness that blended into a single rank wet smell.

We must have looked like a troupe of mimes. Not a sound from us, only the river, red and muddy, softly gurgling at the roots of overturned trees and the stray snags of trees already rotted and sunk in the deep mud. Silently we gathered wood and lighted the chunk of rich, lighter pine John had brought from under the porch. The wood caught. And we all sat on the white strip of sand.

Here the decrepit river was wide, three hundred feet, and here was one of the few places the old thing was at all straight. But for three or four miles, as it forked to surround the long diamond shape of Pine Island, this eastern fork was perfectly straight. At both ends, coming into and out of the fork, it coiled back on itself and looped and squirmed.

The lighter pine sweated its sap and fumed and fussed. Its odor like a concentrate of the woods around us. J. L. yawned. Tom traced with a stick in the pearly sand. Began trickling it through his fingers. Some fell to the ground but the rising wind down the river channel took most of it away.

They talked old times. Told old stories. Tried, it seemed, to recapture themselves as they were in those photographs. But they failed. Those days now far off and as foreign as another language. Tom turned away from the fire, the smoke had begun to drift in his face. "Poor Edie."

"Let's see if any of my trotlines are still out." John rose but the comfortable fire kept everyone else. He touched my shoulder. "Come on, we'll drag the boat down and paddle it. River's calm, the current'll be easy. The motor's at home. Come on."

I nodded, Mother looked across the yellow fire at me. His two brothers looked up at us but were silent.

"We're going in. The mosquitoes are getting bad." Mother stood and brushed off her dress.

We pulled the flatbottom boat smoothly over the mat of pine straw, the noise like fingernails scraping at the shiny metal. From the first John had a definite idea because he had me paddle hard and quickly upstream to where, in the dark, the spidery shapes of limbs, black against the black night, proved to be the swamped trunk of a red oak. He tied his end of the boat off. We were almost in the middle of the river. Below us we could make out the faces of his two brothers against the yellow light of the smoking fire. The smoke rising straight and then, above the treetops, fanning out in the open air. To our right the solid wall of trees on Pine Island. Here, in the open, under the diffused light of the Milky Way, I felt less nervous. The sounds of the river pulling at the old trees were comforting for some reason. We couldn't see one another, two dark shapes only a few feet apart, but I could see, from there, that the two on the beach weren't talking.

"I'm going to close the house." The words out of the dark and barely overcoming the rivernoises. And the dull far-off sound of an owl.

"And do what?"

"Move down here."

"What about Belle?"

"Send her to the state school. They'll be good to her there."

Slowly and then quickly, the moon came up. Just over the trees. Full but flat on one side as if it'd been dropped.

"She did find money." His voice dipping so low that a few times the river choked it off. "Four thousand dollars. Four thousand. All those years of doing for me. Never a spiteful word between us. Everyone knows that, no matter what they say. Escape money she called it. But why so much? I can understand money for this and that. Keeping a little secret just to have some. But four thousand dollars. . ."

On the white blaze of sand the fire had died low, a single spurt of blue flame now and then. J. L. stood looking out over the water and Tom'd lain back on his side, curled around the fire.

"I'll use it to send her away."

Then, the moon directly over us, he told me about the night he found her dying on the couch. The gurgle coming out of the dark then like the rivernoise all around us. Told about the torn foot on the pavement, the black grit rubbed deep into the flesh. And he cried more to himself than out loud. Motionless, I kept my eyes on his brothers and listened until finally, I reached out and touched his knee.

"Listen to me. Listen. Let me tell you why my father never fished." He stopped and in a moment laughed so softly that the current carried it quickly away. Snorted the snort of me and my father—of us—and for a long time we didn't speak.

"Tomorrow night we'll go coon hunting with the dogs. We'll cross over to the island."

"I don't know." I shook my head.

We untied the boat and paddled noisily downstream. The current pushing us on, the island to our right. Coming abreast of his brothers he suddenly yelled and broke the deep quiet of the bottom, scaring a big bird, maybe a roosting owl, that flew moonward over the treetops. J. L. halloed back and Tom, startled by the noise, rose on an elbow and waved weakly.

"What about them?" I asked.

We stopped paddling the awkward boat and drifted. "They don't hunt."

Behind me I heard him rest his paddle on the metal sides and over my shoulder I saw that the delicate man was looking back over his shoulder at the two we'd passed by.

"Maybe tomorrow night."

"What?" He turned to face me. In the silver light his face seemed washed clean.

"Maybe we'll go hunting tomorrow night."

He snorted. "We'll have to tie the dogs in good."

We nodded at one another.

The Necropolis at Savoca

ALL morning long—since
the dimness in the second-class carriage had changed to pink
and then to rose and finally to white—Margaret had battled
silently, privately, with her pain. And during all of this she
had carefully avoided watching Ben, her husband, sketch. It
seemed to her that his rapid, sure strokes made her quiet combat even more difficult. It somehow intensified the already
razor-sharp pains. She had always been irritated by his jerky
sureness—that very paradox itself annoying. But now, with the
heat finally steady and the sunlight full, her pain had quickly
subsided and had brought on an almost ludicrous desire for
a few fresh magazines. Or even for a sudden change in the
angle of the light that would throw some different perspective
on the three pictures that were tacked under glass a few inches
over his head and which were so familiar to her now it seemed
she had known them intimately.

They were black-and-white prints of Sicily's jagged landscape. The first one was of a pebble beach. The distant ship's
sail in it still and stiff, the hull just over the horizon. The second of the Greek ruins at Agrigento. The white columns in
the picture's bright sunlight like the bleached shells of beached
marine creatures. Only the picture of Mt. Etna still held any
of her attention at all. It had held it even through the most

violent spasms suffered in quiet in the heat and stuffiness before her husband's quickly moving hand and occasional upward glance. The mountain's slopes were straight—almost vertical, it seemed. Even in the poor photograph the mountain seemed miraculously cool, the snow laid gently, carefully, on its steep sides. Besides, she'd had a dream about it only last night, hours after she'd heard him come in from some bar. The smell of beer preceding him to bed. Its pungency enough to half-awaken her, enough to cause only the faintest memories of the dream to linger. She had been running through the icy snow near the mountain's summit, near where the slopes drop into the cauldron of the volcano's insides. And there was someone else there, too. Another woman watching her, but only the other woman's eyes moved as she ran quickly past her, her own feet crunching through the thin crust of ice. She plunged past the other woman, sinking to her hips in the coolness, and although the other woman wasn't her mother and wasn't moving her lips at all, the whole dream was full of a song her mother had once sung to her when she was little. The words of it undistorted by the soothing, numbing coolness of the clean, clear air.

"Are you alright?" Ben asked.

She nodded and wiped the sweat from her forehead with an already damp, wilted handkerchief. Even though they'd carefully planned this trip so that they would be traveling to Rome in the cool of early spring, the weather had tricked them from the beginning. That's why, during their two-day stay in Catania to the south, at the very base of the volcano, she had repeatedly begged him to take her up to the mountaintop, to the snow. She wanted to travel up to the coolness, up the road that cut back and forth across the mountain's face at an almost unbelievable angle. But he had shied away, downplayed the heat and stayed, instead, with a political cartoon he was mailing off to a magazine. She'd thought it was a wise-assed panel as she watched him drawing in the hills behind his character's back.

"Please."

He had looked up crossly but immediately smiled. "Maybe later?"

"It would get us out of this awful heat."

"It's not that bad, is it?"

"I guess not." She had sat on their bed, her side turned toward him. "It just seems to bring out the worst smells here."

"Sanitation's bad," he said as he turned back to his cartoon.

"Shouldn't we phone Rome to be sure they're ready when we get there? They said we might do that; this new chemotherapy's pretty complex, remember?"

But when she had seen his back tense involuntarily, she had changed the subject.

She absentmindedly wiped at her forehead again and then folded the handkerchief carefully and laid it on the seat at her side.

"You're sure you're okay?"

"Sure." He was a bright-eyed, nervous man. That's how she described him to herself when they were apart. A pleasant face. Perhaps a bit too long and too square. But she liked it. She even, at times, enjoyed looking straight into his eyes made owlish by the glasses. Except they seldom met eyes now. If it hadn't been for the blank pages of a fairly fresh pad, he'd have been up and out in the vestibule studying a map, clicking a lock back and forth on the restroom door, or swaying with the motion of the train, his elbows on the top of an opened window.

"You need anything?" His bright eyes glanced away from her face and out to the rocky coastline. The train engine ahead sounded its low, moaning whistle and just inches from their window another train lunged past, causing them both to be looking back into their compartment — Ben at his own reflection in the glass with her gaze on the back of his head.

"I think I'll walk down for a glass of beer. Wanta come?" He didn't look around as he spoke. Instead, they both watched the other train. For an instant the two trains were synchronized and they could see, as if they all were perfectly motionless, figures on the southbound train. Standing. Or leaning forward. Someone gesturing to a compartment full of other Sicilians. A party of what looked to be German or Austrian mountaineers. And then, the final image — which remained on their retinas like the afterimage of an extinguished light — a cowled Franciscan bent low over someone lying on a seat; only the expensive woven leather sandals told anything about the prone figure. Then the train passed on, leaving the two in the small compartment a view of the glossy sea, the rocky coastline.

They both sighed softly. She realized that they'd been quite motionless, absolutely still, that her face had become rigid, masklike.

He grinned and reached across to pat her gingerly on the knee. Her skin crawled a bit from the touch as it often did now when he condescended, patronized her with a casual touch due to some eagerness on his part, some vague unexpressed feeling of his that remained mute and self-sustained.

"No," she said.

"'No,' what, Maggie?"

"No, I don't believe I'll go for a beer. Not now, anyway. I'll just thumb through these once more." She waved her hand over the small pile of dog-eared magazines.

"Okay, I'll be right back." Ben stood.

"Don't hurry. No need to." But she involuntarily caught at his hand — grabbed it. He raised her hand and massaged it with his own soft hand, smudged in its creases from the charcoal.

"Bring you anything?"

"No, I'm fine. I ate a ton of those cookies this morning, remember?" She screwed her face up comically.

He laughed and opened the door. For an instant, as he slid the glass door open, she heard the sounds of voices in the vestibule. Disconnected, bodiless voices. A laugh. The sing-song of Sicilian with its harsh edges. And she smelled the strong, choking smell of the cigarettes from next door. But then he closed the door tightly and was off down the hall. She watched him out of sight, his skinny body swaying from wall to wall, his clothes neat and well-fitted. He'd been sitting for a long time, so he moved stiffly, his hand behind him, gouging vehemently at the small of his back.

Alone, she reached for the sketchpad he'd left on the seat and in doing so she leaned forward and touched her chest to her knees.

"God." She almost gasped, then straightened quickly, the sketchpad forgotten in her fingers. She sat back straight against the hard seat as if the pain had returned. But that wasn't it at all. She'd only noticed again that now, when she bent forward, there were no breasts to flatten out on her knees, there was nothing now but the hard, unyielding cage of her ribs, the flat septum, the long welts of the scars themselves.

And all of that moment went to say one single thing to her in the steady heat, in that cloying atmosphere: "I'm going to die." She spoke it aloud as she'd taught herself to do whenever she was reminded by some movements of her own body, by the movements of other women's bodies, by memories or reflections. An ambulance, howling at night, could do it. Or the red cross on a poster.

"I'm going to die," she repeated. The train sped through a crossing and she noticed a line of small cars behind the lowered striped barrier.

She slowly relaxed as best she could in the heat, lay back

heavily against the seat and opened the pad, folded over the sketches she'd already seen, and glanced over the others. But they were all the same. Always, when he wasn't really busy on the single-panel political cartoons that were his real work, he sketched landscapes. He never painted them, though. He always left them in the soft, wavering lines of charcoal.

He just sketched on and on. Over and over the same landscapes. Hills in the background no matter what was daubed lightly in the foreground. Hills that rolled up heavily against one another. Round gentle curves. The very lines of the compositions themselves blurred with the deft stroke of a fingertip.

She knew they were the hills near and beyond his parents' old farm. Those hills full of color, turning from blue mist in the middle distance to an almost violent purple in the far distance before they and the horizon became indistinguishable.

"It's my therapy," he'd told her once. After the death of his parents—their car terribly mangled by a freight train at a crossing, practically rolled up into a nice, tight bundle by the locomotive and then sheared into even pieces by the iron wheels—he'd concentrated on hills.

She idly fingered the rough edges of the paper. When he told her, she'd known immediately that those hills weren't really therapeutic at all. Through those sketches, he'd managed for years to carry their deaths with him without confronting them. She knew that he should have mourned openly and fully and then left it behind with the twisted violence of the car that was towed in and parked up against a nearby service station. She also knew it was a strange memorial. And in that small, tight room, she was afraid she might become such a memory. Some almost automatic gesture with a small daub of charcoal: a single shading here, a stroke there. Never realized and therefore unfinished.

The rattle of the sliding door jerked her back from her thoughts.

"Here, Maggie, I brought you something." He handed her a cheese pastry wrapped in greasy white butcher's paper and a warm bottle of beer. He reached down as he sat and pulled the sketchpad away so that she would have a place for the food.

"I'm hot. Would you . . . ?" She waved the pastry.

He nodded and stood to pull down the window. With the window opened, their place filled with outside noises. There was the bass hum of the electric whistle at crossings. The groan of the carriage's springs as it leaned into the curves. She studied the early green outside that was almost too much to look at. Too verdant. Too tangled and rampant.

The unexpected dull taste of the beer made her grimace. "This beer's flat. Here, taste."

He reached across, the pad still on his lap. "Jesus Christ, it is bad. Tastes worse than flat."

"I don't think so."

"I think it's gone bad. Sorry, I'll get you another; make them take this one back."

"Don't be silly. I've already gobbled down the pie. I'm fine."

He had already stood, his hand on the door handle.

She realized that she'd reached out and grabbed the bottle from him. "No, I'm fine. See, I've still got a half-bottle of mineral water." And she reached with her other hand to uncover it from underneath the magazines. "See, I'm really fine."

"Bastards." He sat back down. "Selling lousy beer to tourists." He bit his lip, cut himself short, and she turned to her magazines.

They were silent for a long time. The train tracks were straight and only a hundred yards from the sea, and the mountains had swung out of view for a while so that now they traveled right at sea level across a flat plain broken only by rubble and trash and the brown, sere beach plants. The sky was cloudless.

Often she almost caught the eye of someone passing in front of their glass windows that opened onto the hallway. She had heard some people speaking English and she would have liked to talk to someone, to pass some time in idle tourist conversation. But whenever she happened to look up, hoping to catch an eye, the person avoided her, looked quickly away. She wondered if the morning's pain had left its mark on her. Was she pale?

A couple of times she did manage to make eye contact and to nod and smile and the other person did the same, but she couldn't tell who could or couldn't speak English and so continued to divide her time between watching the passing people and the magazines.

After a long time she realized she was flipping through the magazines quite oblivious to them, her mind registering only the bright colors of the ads. Across from her Ben stretched like a comfortable cat and rested his head on a hand in preparation for a nap. Suddenly she was restless and sweaty. Her skin felt both hot and clammy simultaneously. She was sure it wasn't the pain returning, but she could hear the throb of her heart in her ear and grew afraid, although she knew it was ridiculous, that he might hear it too.

"They didn't have any cold beer in the dining car?" She was aware that she'd spoken too loudly.

Ben opened his eyes quickly and straightened in his seat as if he were embarrassed she had caught him dozing. "No, they didn't have anything cold at all. Seems someone forgot to fix the refrigerators this morning. Typical, huh?"

She was irritated and only stared at him. "I've been having pains."

"What?" He leaned forward and reached for her knee,

his hand coming to rest heavily on it. She could feel its coolness through the thin cotton skirt.

"Santa Teresa, five minuti." The conductor opened and shut the door with a vengeance.

Margaret shifted in her seat in order to collect the scattered magazines and in doing so moved her knee out from under his touch.

They both rose and stood back to back, fumbling with their luggage.

"Only minor ones. Small pains." She could hear him behind her opening the clasps on his suitcase, packing away his sketchpad. She was sorry that she'd said anything.

"Maybe it's your period. Couldn't that be it?"

"Sure. That's probably what it is. It's about that time." As she stretched her arms for the plastic bags full of fruit on the very top rack, she felt the slight tug of resistance under her arms and down her chest and then the few remaining muscles took their cue and began to function.

Santa Teresa was dreary. A dirty, working town of two or three thousand bordered on both the north and south by open gravel pits that not only provided almost everyone with some form of employment but also managed to cover the tables in the cafés, the hotel foyers, the people in the streets with a patina of white, pearly dust. True, she had been deceived at first from the distance. A mile out, the town promised some shady coolness—an escape from the heat that seemed to have followed them everywhere the last three weeks. A warped, distorted perspective even promised to place the small town amongst the gently rolling foothills her husband sketched so frequently, but it cheated. It was only a shabby, dusty, poor sort of place.

"Look," Ben said. He had already found a small church as they emerged from the cavernous train station. It was white-washed and devoid of the usual gaudy ornamentation.

"A thousand and one." She still carried some anger from the train.

"What?" They stopped to readjust the baggage that had already eaten red grooves into their hands.

"That makes a thousand and one white churches we've seen so far."

He had left the suitcases and was headed toward the church, but he turned toward her once he'd crossed the street. "Come on, be a sport."

"No." She was irritated by the grit between her teeth. "I'm tired of them and museums and statues and illuminated manuscripts and . . ." The words hurried out.

He shrugged and crossed the street and picked up his suitcase. They walked on, forced to keep their eyes open for the dog shit that had puddled here and there.

"They must all own St. Bernards," she said.

"Horses." He smiled at her. "Let's stop before we look for a hotel. Okay?"

They sat at a small table covered by a bright red-and-blue Cinzano awning. They were the only customers. She noticed that even the flies, which accompanied the lazy waiter out from the darkness of the interior, seemed uninterested in them and quickly retreated.

"Two beers." Ben held up two fingers, practically his only form of communication with the Sicilians.

The waiter took awhile and when he returned he thumped the bottles down and quickly returned to the shade.

"At least they aren't flat," she said.

"Yeah."

They drank for a while, the beer gritty though neither wanted to mention it.

"Are you okay?"

"Sure," she said.

He nodded at her and held up two fingers.

"No, this is fine."

"Come on. Let's get ripped."

"I don't think so. It's too hot and we've got a hotel to find, remember?"

The hotel they finally decided on, after checking almost all the town had to offer, was fairly nice. The old parquet floor in their one small room had come unstuck years ago and now clattered when they crossed it. They had bathed, eaten, and walked with the rest of the inhabitants on their promenade— their *passeggiata*. Walked, with the entire town, from gravel pit to gravel pit. Now he lay on the bed, the pillows folded under his head, idly running a felt-tipped pen across some hotel paper.

"Tomorrow we'll hitch up into the hills above here," he said. "They say some of the smaller villages are nice."

"They said that about here too, didn't they?" She sat combing her short hair before the dull mirror whose edges had blurred and frosted with age. The yellow light was at her back. She wiped a thin line of sweat from her forehead.

"Well, the old piazza is nice."

"Four hundred and ten."

"Don't start that again."

"Just a joke." She could see him in the mirror. She noticed that he'd filled an entire page with the soft swelling curves of his hills. "Stop that."

"What?" He looked up in alarm as she took a shaky sip of the thick, sweet Marsala.

"That goddamned doodling you do. Let's go out on the balcony and have a drink. 'Get ripped,' as you say."

"Are you kidding? That awful stuff." He made a face. "I'll run down for a paper. From Rome. We can see what's up in the way of movies, plays. *Grand opera.*" He boomed out the last words.

Methodically she finished her hundred strokes and walked, with her wine, out to the iron chair on the miniature balcony. "A paper?" she said back into the room.

"Why not?"

She took another sweet taste and began to feel it between her eyes. "I phoned Rome this afternoon."

"Oh." He stopped tying his shoelace.

"The doctor said they were ready for us anytime. They can start the chemotherapy as soon as we arrive."

"Well, that's good, isn't it? It's what we've hoped for."

She nodded as he bent back over. "Absolutely."

She kept pouring herself glasses after he had left. She'd been drinking the syrup for a long time when the first pain came on. "No." She spoke aloud to the empty room behind her. It's only the wine rumbling in my stomach, she told herself but knew it wasn't. "They lied." Again she spoke. This time recalling how the doctors, all of them, had lied to her from the very first about the pain. "Don't worry," they said. "It'll never be bad, not at all really bad. There are drugs now. God, you should have seen the way it used to be."

But their drugs proved useless and she no longer took them. She knew by now the best way to meet the pain, so she crawled slowly from the chair, not wanting to antagonize it further, onto her hands and knees, and then dropped onto her stomach with both her hands up under her, just below her navel. Now she was ready, except that she was afraid of it and also she was afraid Ben might come back any moment to see her lying prone on the small balcony. "God, please don't let him come in and see me," she said over and over like some strange incantation. Suddenly the pain intensified and as it did she dug, gouged savagely at herself with both her fists.

She pushed back at the pain as if it were something other than her own insides. She fought with her fists against it, too busy even to cry out, too occupied to do anything but struggle and sweat.

For a long time afterwards, she lay motionless on the rough floor, her face pressed to the damp iron bars of the railing. She breathed shallowly, afraid that any movement might bring it all back again. Below, three old men tried to sell the last of their day's catch, but by now no one wanted the fish. Even though she was high up and across the street from the vendors, she could smell the salty sweetness of the tuna. Finally, she crawled over to the bed.

After the pain, nothing mattered. Not even his seeing her. Not a single thing mattered. As she lay naked, having carefully, skillfully removed her clothes with her fingertips, she felt washed clean of everything. Still, as she gently bent over to turn off the light, she hoped she might again dream her dream. Her feet almost flying from under her as she ran, almost fell, down the steep slopes of snow, away from the volcano's core. The other woman watching her intently from under dark hair. The dream full of quiet—in the way the snowdrifts angled against themselves, in the subtle change in the color of the snow from white to blue where the shadows fell across it—and full of noise, too. Loud with the words of her mother's song: *Keep those cold, icy fingers off of me.* She remembered how her mother, just come in from an early morning laundry, would run her cool but soothing hands up under the warm pile of quilts and over the childish, flat chest to tickle her awake.

She lay an hour or more in the heat, desiring the numbing cold of the dream, but she decided she might want it too much and that she might keep it away by being too expectant. So, she tried to think of something else and finally, long before Ben came in, she drifted off into a deep, dreamless sleep.

II

THE small car swerved quite dramatically out of the traffic and slid to a stop almost on their toes.

"Oh boy," Ben muttered loudly.

The young man motioned for them to hop over the door whose handle was wired shut with an electrical cord, a plug still dangling from one end.

"Savoca?" she asked as Ben crowded her up against the man's garish plaid jacket.

"Sì, Savoca." He turned to smile at her, his teeth an even, dun-colored line. He added something else she wasn't able to understand and, still smiling, swerved back into the traffic and toward the full round hills that lay gently one against the other up above Santa Teresa.

The man's sharp cologne almost nauseated her. Below his ear she noticed a black scrap of toilet paper he'd used to stanch a shaving nick. And she quickly looked away when she realized that the blood had begun to seep out again, forming a small bright red droplet. He had been watching her peripherally and smiled as he turned toward her, carelessly forcing the old yellow Fiat around the tight curves. "Why Savoca?"

She shrugged good-naturedly and nodded toward Ben, who was idly playing with the electrical plug that rattled in the wind against the side of the car.

"Arance." The driver indicated the trees that covered the slopes above them and that fell away sharply to their right.

"Oranges?"

"Sì, oranges."

Some pickers were in the groves, up under the dark shade of the trees. On the steep slopes they had no choice but to fill long bags full of the fruit and then, two or three strong, pull and push them up the precipitous incline to the road. The driver came dangerously close to some of the pickers who were loading the bags of fruit into a small truck. He blared his horn at them and laughed.

"I guess I don't need this." She pulled at the sleeve of Ben's loose brown windbreaker she was wearing.

He looked at her out of the corner of his eye. "No, it's too late for the cold up here. It's been an early summer, I think."

He dropped them off in the small piazza and sped off up the hill, never looking back but casually waving over his shoulder and controlling the skid of the car calmly with one hand. She wondered, watching him, if maybe he were headed up toward the mountain. Surely it was cooler up there.

They stood alone on the dirty uneven stones of the piazza, splotched by years of discarded trash. Spilled oil, mashed insects. The stones, loose under their step, moved as they crossed to the small empty fountain. Even though at this height the air was lighter and thinner, there wasn't a hint of a breeze. The caper bushes by the sides of doorways were still. Everything was too still, she thought. Like a carefully planned ambush in the movies. Surely from between closed shutters they were being watched. Dark eyes in leathery faces gleaming because they were crossed by a single bright bar of light.

"Siesta time," Ben said.

"Guess so. What's to see?"

Ben took out an old brochure he had picked up at the newspaper stand in Santa Teresa. He thumbed through its yellowed pages.

"A church."

"Oh great, just great."

"Oh come on."

"Here." She began peeling off the windbreaker as he put one leg up on the rim of the fountain. As she was pulling off the last sleeve, a figure suddenly appeared in a doorway across the street from them. It was only the dim shape of a man.

A thin figure, only his knees and legs clearly showing in the brilliant afternoon light, his upper body in deep shade. He motioned for them or seemed to because he waved only once, a brief peremptory sort of motion, and disappeared back inside.

"At least there's someone here," she said.

"Where?" Ben had been looking toward where the piazza jutted out over the valley below.

"Over there in the bar." She folded the jacket under her arm.

They crossed the street and passed behind a truck filled with oranges. Some of the fruit had rolled out onto the cobblestones and lay smashed and sour. They stepped around the dark puddles of colored pulp.

"Come in, come in, my friends."

Their eyes didn't adjust for a few seconds. The interior was blindingly dark and they both squinted their eyes. Hers corrected first and she pulled him after her by the hand.

"Hello," she said. She could make out the figure.

"Hello to you, lady." The thin man behind the bar wore the same sort of blue dirty coveralls that clothed almost the entire working population of the island. "You want drink, eh?"

"Sì, sure." Ben turned to her inquiringly. But she was too busy ranging her eyes over the place, over the dust-covered bottles of sweet vermouths, sweet liqueurs. Amongst them the air seemed to break in tangible waves like the fractured air over an expanse of desert floor. She was disappointed that this place wasn't cool.

"What, please?"

"Campari? Yes, that's it. Two bitter Campari. Due."

"Due Campari."

She noticed that the light from the street, softened somehow by the dust all around them, made Ben's thick glasses shine with a red tint.

"Where is everybody?" Ben asked.

"Gone."

"Gone?"

"Sì, yes, here and there. You know how it is, surely. People come and go, eh?" He nodded. "The young go to the coast to catch fish, to picnic with their lives. The others, like my sons, go down everyday just to pick, and to drink at somebody else's bar. The old. . ." He had filled the glasses full of the bittersweet drink. "Sorry, no ice today, eh?"

"This is fine."

"Fine for you too, lady?"

She said it was, noticing, as she took her drink, how long his fingernails were. How they curved inward, curled long and yellow around the curve of the glass itself.

"The old they go up to the necropolis."

"The what?" Ben asked, his drink halfway to his lips.

"The necropolis. You don't have that word, necropolis?"

"I don't."

"That's too bad. A fine old word." The large sleeves that swallowed his wrists swept across the top of the bar as he gestured. "They die, the old do. Like me."

"Like you?" Ben drank watching the thin old man.

"Sì, yes, I'm eighty-seven."

"No."

"Oh sì, yes. Eighty-seven." He touched his shiny pomaded hair with a single long fingernail. "Not a drop of dye. Still as black as it was seventy years ago." He winked at Ben. "You want to see it?"

Ben glanced at her, his eyeglasses flashing. "See what?"

"Why, the necropolis. People come from the whole world wide to see it. From Chicago. Gangsters, I think. We talk, they have a drink, we go up the hill. All simple, eh? Maybe they buy a postcard, maybe not." He motioned over his shoulder to a wire rack full of glossy rectangles. The actual pictures were indiscernible in the thick darkness of their corner.

"A cemetery?" Ben asked.

She felt him staring at her but she was looking instead at the postcards.

"You don't, do you?" he asked, touching her shoulder.

She looked up full into his face but the bad light and his glasses kept their eyes apart. "Why not? Sure. We haven't seen a single one of those yet, have we?"

Ben drank and motioned for another.

"Why else come here?" The old man poured out the second glass.

"The church?"

The old man made a clicking sound in his throat. A rattle, deep, almost in his lungs. It was a dry, hollow sound. "It's nothing. Besides, you can see it. It's near the necropolis. Right up the hill, eh?"

Ben laid some coins down. "I don't think so, not today. Maybe some other time."

"I'll be joyful to take you there." The old man wiped the glasses off cursorily and turned his back to them to fumble under the postcard rack.

"I don't think so, thanks anyway."

"Is it cool there?" she asked.

Ben turned to her. The old man looked up and spoke to her in the dull mirror. "No, lady, I'm sorry."

She nodded slowly. "Come on, Ben, be a sport."

Ben shook his head quickly and spoke to the old man's reflection. "We can manage. Just point us in the right direction."

"Oh no, I have the keys. I'm the mayor, Niccolò Peretti." He again stroked his slick hair with the palm of his hand.

"Keys?"

"Oh sì, yes, it's always locked. A national treasure. Built in the 1600s by the Franciscans out of solid granite . . . scusi, excuse me, I'll wait for that, eh?"

"Locked?" Ben took her arm and turned her to face him, but the old man was already around the bar and framed by the door, silhouetted by the bright light through the doorway, motioning for them to follow. Outside, behind him, she saw some oranges lose their hold and roll from the truck to split open on the street.

"Come on. Come on." She patted his arm.

As they passed into the light following Niccolò Peretti, she noticed the swarm of blue-black flies all over the split fruit. She could hear their constant drone even after they had passed by.

They climbed up a side street at a sharp angle, following the narrow road their driver had taken. She turned once to look back and down to the cluster of dull white houses and out to the valley. The sea beyond was a delicate blue line on the horizon. She was very sorry that she couldn't see Mt. Etna from here. She would have given almost anything for even the slightest, briefest view of its snowy slopes.

The two men had stopped farther up to wait for her. Ben was anxious, his hand tapping at the small, rolled-up sketchpad in his back pocket. She felt a gentle tug at her bowels. Like the slow bite of a trout she'd once caught as a child.

She massaged her stomach surreptitiously under the jacket draped over one arm, as she climbed behind them to where the street leveled off a bit, for fifty yards or so, before it began to ascend even more sharply and disappeared into the dark of a thick stand of pines.

"The church, eh?" The thin old man waved vaguely toward one side of the road, his long fingernails catching the late afternoon light.

The church wasn't much. Once it might have been worth a tourist's detour up from the coastal highway, but now it was hardly more than a pile of rubble.

"The Germans," the old man said, motioning over his shoulder, refusing even to turn—the church was worth so little of his attention.

Ben studied his brochure while she walked over some of the loose stones, her footing unsure, to pick a few leaves off a clump of rosemary.

"The necropolis, eh?" Niccolò Peretti slouched across the narrow street to a single doorway set back a few feet into a stone building like a blockhouse. The building was low, squat. Not a single piece of ornamentation broke the dreary faded blue of the wall. It had only one wooden door and doorframe. He fumbled with the keys, mumbling to himself.

"This is the cemetery?" Ben's voice, she noticed, was lower than usual. But she had to ignore him in preparation for the pain she was certain would come soon. She rubbed the small tight seed of it under the windbreaker.

"Necropolis. *Necropolis*. You must learn the word, eh?"

"Are you . . . ?"

"Yes, yes." She spoke through clenched teeth.

The old man had managed to joggle the key in the lock in some secret combination of twists and jerks and turned to look up at Ben. "What's the matter? If you don't like, you don't have to tip, eh? Come see if you like. Come on. Don't disappoint the lady." He had opened the door and stood just inside.

The three of them began to descend the flight of stairs. The dim light at the bottom was full of the dust they kicked up. The light rebounded off the terra cotta floor and met them coming down in a transformed ochre haze.

Ben stopped suddenly, but she gently, wordlessly, edged around him and went down to where the man stood at the bottom of the staircase looking up. She descended slowly, her arms outstretched, her hands sliding easily down the painted walls. As she stepped down, the room below was filled in from the bottom upwards. At first all she could see was the scratched surface of the terra cotta floor. And all she could smell was the fusty attic smell of dryness and slow decay.

But the pairs of feet startled her. Three which became four and then five and then six as she descended. The cracked shoes giving way gradually to thin calves covered with knee socks, the material fuzzy in the hot yellow light. The layer of dust on the cloth shone like gilt.

"This isn't a cemetery," Ben said. She barely heard his voice coming from behind and above her.

On the last steps she came even with the faces themselves. The skin shot through with dust, somehow the texture of it the essence of dryness and heat, causing her throat to close. The eye sockets empty, the flesh puckered around their edges. The tight unyielding skin of the forehead seemed, in the light, to glow as if it were hot from fever. The coarse, brittle hair, dull and frazzled lay in scattered clumps on the scalps. The bodies, the walls, the heat, the dusty floor, the very air too dry to breathe, dry enough to choke her, quickly and utterly to shut her throat.

"Maggie." Ben's voice reverberated down the staircase but she had already given the old man her hand.

He dragged her after him as he made a circuit of the room, motioning vehemently with his other hand, taking her up close to the faces. "Here, this is Dottore Cerrata," he said and pulled her near the hollow chest, the gaping jaws that lay open like a trap. But she looked down, at their feet, rubbing viciously at the pain, trying to conjure up some part of her dream. The snow almost captured but disappearing, as if it were melting away.

"Ah, Signora Ongaro. Bella. Look up, lady." His Sicilian began to break up the sentences.

Margaret began to realize, with his fingernails digging painfully into her palm, how idle and foolish her dream had been, and suddenly the pain took hold, came on in an increasing swell.

"Look. Signora Ongaro. Bella. Molto bella, eh?"

Margaret forced herself to look into the desiccated face of the woman before her.

"Here." The old man firmly took her hand from where it clutched her stomach and stretched it out full length to touch the dead woman's cheek. Maybe it was an illusion caused by the pain she could no longer massage, but Margaret thought she could feel just the slightest hint of softness lingering somewhere behind the awful rigidity of the ancient skin stretched drum-tight over the protruding cheekbones.

She tried to recall through the crescendo of pain and the old man's words the soothing lyrics of her mother's song, but as they moved from figure to figure his broken English gave way to full Italian and the cadence of it became the very tempo of her mother's voice until the Sicilian absorbed it, cleared it from her mind. And yet, the unintelligible words weren't unsettling. Not at all. Instead they were like some love song fast but melodious.

The three of them were like a tableau. Like action frozen in the chiaroscuro of the dust. Ben had halted on the last step, unable to make the final move to the terra cotta floor. The old man and the woman were caught before a single figure wired securely into its safe dry niche. The wire run under the arms and back to bolts cemented into the wall. The old man's arm almost stroking the parchment skin, her body bent in a gentle curve as if she were slowly succumbing to gravity and would presently, when the action resumed, sink down to the warm tiles as soundlessly as one of the hollow figures would if a wire snapped, if it broke and unraveled from around the shoulders.

And over it all there was the old man's melody, the beautiful meaningless words in strange sympathy with the intense heat, the swirling dust in the pale light, the audience of the dead.

About the Author

Born in Lufkin, Texas, in 1951, James Hannah earned both a B.S. and an M.A. from Stephen F. Austin State University and an M.F.A. from the University of Iowa Writers' Workshop. He has taught at Texas A&M University and now teaches at Murray State University in Kentucky, where he lives with his wife, Cecelia Hawkins, and their two children, Elizabeth and Sarah.

Mr. Hannah was a finalist in the Associated Writing Programs Award Series in Short Fiction in 1982, and stories by him have twice been nominated for Pushcart Prizes. Most recently he has been awarded a National Endowment for the Arts Creative Writing Fellowship for 1988.